THE CONCISE
VISITOR'S GUIDE TO
YELLOWSTONE

Although the author and publisher have made every effort to ensure the accuracy of the information in this book, neither party assumes any responsibility for errors, inaccuracies, or injuries resulting from partaking in the activities described herein or by taking the author's advice. It is strongly suggested that you talk with an expert, such as a park ranger, prior to engaging in outdoor activities in any national park.

Readers should be advised that Web sites, phone numbers, and other sources for further information may have changed or disappeared between the time this was written and when it is read.

ISBN: 1453618821
EAN13: 9781453618820
LCCN: 2010908414

THE CONCISE VISITOR'S GUIDE TO YELLOWSTONE

MATT BOLTON

TABLE OF CONTENTS

ACKNOWLEDGEMENTS

I wish to express my thanks to the National Park Service and to Yellowstone National Park for allowing me to use the maps in this book. I also want to acknowledge the NPS.gov Web site as an invaluable resource in gathering specifics on locations, times, contact information, and other specifics used in this book.

Heartfelt thanks go out to my wife, Karen, for her resourcefulness and assistance. Without her, this book would have never gone from an idea to a published reality.

PREFACE

My name is Matt Bolton, and my passion is for our beloved national parks. I am not one of the lucky ones who get to spend their entire lives, day after day, year after year, visiting national parks. I have never been overseas. The only foreign country I have ever had the privilege to visit is Canada, and what a beautiful place our friends to the north have. However, my family and I have made it a goal to visit as many national parks as possible, and along the way, we have been fortunate to visit most of the United States' major national parks, as well as those of western Canada.

I've made multiple trips to Yellowstone National Park (NP) and Grand Teton NP in Wyoming. I have vacationed at Zion NP, Bryce Canyon NP, Arches NP, and Canyonlands NP in Utah. I have visited Yosemite NP, Kings Canyon NP, Sequoia NP, Muir Woods National Monument (NM), Cabrillo NM, Redwood NP, and Point Reyes National Seashore in California. I have visited Olympic NP, North Cascades NP, and Mount Rainier NP in Washington. I've been to Crater Lake NP and Oregon Caves NM in Oregon, as well as both the north and south rims of Grand Canyon NP in Arizona. Other trips have included Rocky Mountain NP, Mesa Verde NP, and the Black Canyon of the Gunnison NP in Colorado, Denali NP and Kenai Fjords NP in Alaska, and Haleakala NP and the USS Arizona Memorial in Hawaii. I've hiked at Glacier NP in Montana, Isle Royale NP in Michigan, Mammoth Cave NP in Kentucky, Indiana Dunes National Lakeshore, Great Smoky Mountain NP in Tennessee and North Carolina, and Gettysburg National Military Park in Pennsylvania. I have driven through the Everglades NP in Florida (too many alligators to hike through the swamps there). Finally, my family and I have also traveled to Waterton Lakes NP, Jasper NP, Glacier NP, Yoho NP, Mount Revelstoke NP, and Banff NP in western Canada. Most of these parks I have visited once; however, I have made multiple visits to Yellowstone, Grand Teton, Yosemite, Rocky Mountain, and Great Smoky Mountain national parks.

In 2009, I published my first book: *The Concise Visitor's Guide to Yosemite*. This book, *The Concise Visitor's Guide to Yellowstone*, is a logical follow-up, bringing together my extensive park experiences along with my recent writing and publishing experience to tackle our nation's very first and most famous national park: Yellowstone.

This in no way makes me an expert. If you want an expert, talk to a park ranger at any of the parks. They've been trained, schooled, and tested. They are extremely knowledgeable, friendly, and willing to assist anyone. However, if you wish to locate some help in preparing your trip; if you are seeking an honest opinion and candid advice from someone who has vacationed at nearly every major U.S. national park, including multiple trips to Yellowstone; if you are feeling kind of overwhelmed and not sure where to even begin to prepare for your first trip to Yellowstone, then I hope you find this book to be the answer. I hope you find it to be the right thing at the right time to get you feeling properly prepared and somewhat educated on this fantastic place. I have tried my very best in this book to give sage advice, coming from someone who simply loves Yellowstone and has traveled to most all parts of the park on multiple visits.

The concept behind this book is for it to serve as a concise, reliable, and easy-to-use resource. I hope it will assist you with such needs as knowing where to get a meal; understanding why you might choose one day hike over another; knowing where to see the best geysers, mud pots, fumaroles, and hot springs if time does not allow you to visit all areas of this massive park; planning how to spend your evenings; knowing where you might want to book your lodging to be closest to the parts of the park that interest you most; knowing what to do if you encounter wildlife (and you definitely will); knowing how to see the sights by guided tour, making sure your kids have a great time as well; providing the much-needed phone numbers and Web sites; and much more.

Hopefully, you will get something out of this book that always makes me envious: a well-planned and great trip to Yellowstone.

INTRODUCTION

This is the second book I've written; the second book on one of our most stunning national parks. In 2009, I wrote and published *The Concise Visitor's Guide to Yosemite.* Yellowstone is quite different, unique, and unbelievably special in numerous ways. It has the distinction of being not only the first national park in the United States, but also the first in the world. It is not only a place of unbelievable beauty, containing more than half of the worlds geysers, but is also (along with nearby Grand Teton National Park) the very best national park for viewing and coming in close contact with some of our most revered wildlife. The Yellowstone/Grand Teton area has the greatest concentration and variety of wildlife in the United States outside of Alaska; specifically, it has one of the largest numbers of elk in the world and is one of the few remaining homes to grizzly bear in the lower forty-eight states. Perhaps more than any other place in the country, Yellowstone is the first place one thinks of when discussing the American bison. Bison (commonly referred to as buffalo) have been featured in numerous films and on

xiii

U.S. coins. Yellowstone National Park is the second-largest national park in the lower forty-eight states (Death Valley NP is the largest) with a unique combination of forests, wildlife, thermal activity, and history. Yellowstone is one of the largest active volcanoes in the world and includes the largest high-altitude lake in the world—Yellowstone Lake.

My attempt here is to give advice and suggestions, to give tips from someone who has covered most all of this park on multiple visits. I am not trying to force my opinion on others; you can get books and brochures on Yellowstone from a million different places. They are all good but give basically the same information. They tell you about accommodations, history and geology of the park, where places of interest are located, food options, admission fees, and distances and highlights of hiking trails. What is difficult to find is soundly based, well-researched opinions regarding the many things to do, and from someone who did it the hard way.

I have made multiple trips to this fantastic place and never had anyone advise me on what to see if I had limited time, where to stay, where to get the right food for a hike versus a well-earned, big dinner, or the many other tips that I have included here so that you can get it right the first time. You are probably a person thinking about your first trip to Yellowstone. It seems beautiful and fascinating, yet at the same time, enormous and remote. All of these adjectives are accurate. You probably have a fair amount of apprehension as you try to figure out where to begin. Hopefully, the time you spend absorbing this publication will pay off in the form of a good trip, if not the very best trip of your life. I certainly hope so.

Yellowstone is a place to be inspired, a place to exercise or relax, a place to stand beneath some of the world's most famous (as well as many not so famous) geysers. It is a place to spend time among majestic wildlife, and a place to enjoy food—from fine dining to sub sandwiches. You can hike, watch bison roam in the wild, time the intervals of the geyser eruptions, fish, backpack with llamas, eat fine food, sit beside one of the most beautiful stone fireplaces you'll ever see, and much more. Yellowstone is one of those places you simply must see in your lifetime, hopefully more than once!

I will never forget my parents' visit to Yellowstone National Park. Upon their return, they told me that they had seen Yellowstone; my questioning for details revealed that they had spent a grand total of two hours in the park. My parents are a prime example of well-meaning folks who, unfortunately, have no concept of what the national park experience is really all about. If you see yourself in this same mind-set, then hopefully this publication will open your eyes to the offerings and beauty that is right there for the taking.

As previously mentioned, Yellowstone is the oldest national park in the United States, and the entire world. It set the example for the world and has led countries internationally to set aside their land treasures to be preserved for generations to come. The United States alone as of August 2010 has 392 units or individual sites in its national park system; specifically, there are fifty-eight national parks. Yellowstone was the fifth-most-visited U.S. national park in 2008, following Great Smoky Mountain NP, Grand Canyon NP, Yosemite NP, and Olympic NP. Visitation at Great Smoky Mountain, while it is a beautiful place, would never be more than twice that of the Grand Canyon, in second place, if it were not much more easily accessible and located near the disproportionately more heavily populated eastern United States. The 2009 visitation at

Yellowstone was a record-breaking 3,295,187, according to the National Park Service official statistics; it was the fifth-most visited national park in the United States for that year as well. Visitation has held very consistently around the three million mark since 1990. Climates vary by regions, elevation, and time of year. Wildlife is abundant, including black bear, grizzly bear, bison, elk, gray wolf, and moose. As mentioned previously, Yellowstone is the second-largest national park in the continental United States comprising approximately 3,472 square miles or 2,221,766 acres (larger than Rhode Island and Delaware combined). Yellowstone is sixty-three miles north to south and fifty-four miles wide east to west. While it is thought of as a Wyoming park, small portions of it stretch into Montana (3 percent) to the north and Idaho (1 percent) to the west.

According to the National Park Service, Yellowstone requires approximately eight hundred National Park Service employees (four hundred year-round) and thirty-five hundred concession employees. There are five park entrances, 466 miles of road (310 paved), fifteen miles of boardwalks, ninety-two trailheads, approximately one thousand miles of backcountry trails, and 301 backcountry campsites. There are nine visitor centers, nine hotels or lodges, seven National Park Service-operated campgrounds (450+ sites), and five concession operated campgrounds (1,700+ sites). There are fifty-two picnic areas and one marina. Yellowstone is home to at least sixty-seven species of mammals, over three hundred species of birds, sixteen species of fish, six reptiles, and four amphibians. The only current resident mammal on the threatened species list is the Canada lynx. The gray wolf was removed from the endangered species list then put back on the list in 2008. Since April 1, 2009, its status has not been clear.

Most of the park is actually a volcano, one of the largest active volcanoes in the world. The caldera (or volcanic rim) encompasses much of the park, including many of its most famous features such as the upper, middle, and lower geyser basins, the Grand Canyon of Yellowstone, the Old Faithful Inn Hotel, and most of Yellowstone Lake. Yellowstone experienced an estimated 2,317 earthquakes in 2009 and it is believed that the first Yellowstone eruption occurred nearly 2.1 million years ago and was thought to have been six thousand times the size of the Mount Saint Helens eruption of 1980. There was a second eruption nearly 1.3 million years ago and a third, creating the current caldera, about 640,000 years ago. A much smaller eruption about 174,000 years ago is thought to have created the West Thumb of Yellowstone Lake. Don't worry, scientists constantly monitor this area and are not expecting any future eruptions for at least thousands, if not millions of years!

The Yellowstone Caldera is one of the world's largest, measuring thirty by forty-five miles in size. There exist more than three hundred geysers and approximately ten thousand hydrothermal features. Yellowstone Lake (the largest in the park) has an average depth of fourteen feet, comprises approximately 132 miles of surface area and 141 miles of shoreline. The park has approximately 290 waterfalls!

The lodgepole pine is by far the most common tree in Yellowstone; here they grow up to seventy-five feet tall. They are very shade tolerant and often drop their branches left in the shade below the canopy. Lodgepole pines growing by themselves often have branches all the way to the base of the trunk because the entire tree receives regular sunlight. Also common in Yellowstone are limber pines, whitebark pine, engelmann spruce, subalpine fir, Douglas fir, rocky mountain juniper, cottonwood, and quaking aspen.

Yellowstone's seclusion and relative isolation made it a known beauty only to Native Americans until the early 1800s. Even today, its isolation and distance from major cities and their airports keep this unbelievable place of natural beauty and wonder from being overrun with tourists. You have to actually want to see Yellowstone and make an effort to get there so only the serious vacationers, those who truly appreciate our great national parks, as well as those who truly want to see what they have been missing typically pass through her gates.

It is widely believed that a fur trapper named John Colter was the first Anglo to see what is now called Yellowstone National Park in the winter of 1807–1808. Obviously many Native Americans worked and lived on this land well before this time. The discovery of gold in nearby Montana brought prospectors to the area around 1860. No large gold strikes were ever made in what is officially Yellowstone National Park. The first authorized expedition to come to the area to begin to explore and map the area came in 1860 in the form of a military expedition led by Captain William F. Raynolds. The U.S. government focused its efforts on the Civil War for the next few years and once again, exploration of Yellowstone was basically shelved until the very end of the decade.

On August 20, 1886, the U.S. Army was placed in charge of protecting and administering the park. While the army was very proficient at patrolling and guarding this large land mass, they were not properly trained to answer questions or educate visitors on the history, geography, or geology of the park.

In 1916, Congress passed the National Park Service Organic Act and in doing so, established the National Park Service. This created the structure from which to hire and properly train the first park rangers assigned to Yellowstone. After recruitment and training, the first rangers assumed their posts in 1918 under the guidance of Yellowstone's first superintendent, Horace M. Albright. Legend has it that the Minnetaree tribe residing in the area called the main river flowing through the park the "Mi tse a-da-zi," which roughly translates over to English as "Rock Yellow River." Through the years it was altered to "Yellow Stone" and then into just a single word "Yellowstone."

In this book, I will attempt to give you the skinny on eating, places of interest, activities, preparation, expenses, hiking, wildlife (what to worry about and what not to worry about), basic accommodation advice, and how to open up the world of Yellowstone. Even as a multiple-time visitor to this magnificent place, I've only taken one solid bite out of all Yellowstone has to offer.

Let me also put in a plug here for what an unbelievable bargain Yellowstone or any national park is. The admission fee for Yellowstone is $25. This gets you, your car, and as many people as you can fit into it twenty-four-hour access to both Yellowstone and neighboring Grand Teton NP for a full week. Compare this to the cost of a movie for a family of four, not to mention that most movies these days are disappointing and last around ninety minutes. The national parks are the best value in family fun anywhere.

By the way, accommodations are a bargain as well. This is why they often book up to a year in advance. They do not charge what the market will bear or a fee based upon supply and demand. If they did, they would be far more expensive. They simply charge a bargain fee and let the early planners get them! (More on this fantastic bargain in Chapter Ten.)

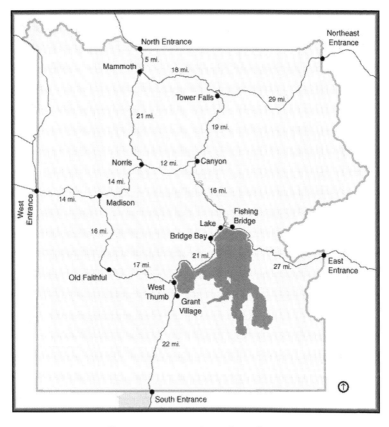

Yellowstone National Park Map

Chapter 1

HOW TO GET TO YELLOWSTONE

T here are two ways to get to Yellowstone. You might live close enough to drive (in which case, I'll let you get out your atlas, as well as admit that I am jealous) or, if you live farther away, you have the choice between a very long tiring road trip and several flight options. First, let me say that it is a good thing that Yellowstone, or really most any of the magnificent large western national parks, are NOT located on the outskirts of large cities. If they were, the crowds would totally ruin a great thing. The fact that it takes some effort to get to places like Yellowstone is a natural selector that limits the crowds and limits the casual sightseers that would, quite frankly, get in the way of those who go there for the right reasons. If you are a regular park-goer, then you know exactly what I mean. If you aren't, but put forth the effort to experience Yellowstone, you will surely find out.

Anyway, the nearest large airport is Salt Lake City, located 372 miles away; a drive of approximately six and one-half hours. I have done this. It is well worth the drive. Salt Lake City, Utah, will give you the most airline selections, the most flight time choices, and usually the best flight and rental car prices. However, several options will get you much closer. Multiple major airlines or their regional connectors serve regional airports in Jackson Hole, Wyoming, and Bozeman and Billings, Montana. These airports will get you to within a few hours' drive, provide rental car facilities, and allow you to spend more of your vacation time in the park. However, be advised that the flight options will not be as great, and expect the prices for both flights and rental cars to be somewhat higher. These airports will also have some seasonality to their schedules and prices, especially Jackson Hole, as this is a major snow ski destination. Also, remember that most roads inside Yellowstone NP are closed to automobiles from November through much of April. Only the north entrance is plowed and only as far south as Mammoth Hot Springs. This may help you make a decision on where you want to fly in to if you are planning a winter visit. Jackson Hole, while a great destination for winter skiing, would not be a good choice for Yellowstone in winter, as you would have to make it all the way around the park on potentially treacherous winter roads to get to the north entrance, since the south entrance glaring at you on your map as the logical way to enter the park would be closed for the season!

There are other regional airport options including Cody, Wyoming; Pocatello, Idaho; and West Yellowstone, Montana. However, they offer limited service and are not something I would generally recommend.

When you arrive, any of these smaller cities would be great places to stock up on a few groceries, film, camera batteries, snow chains, or anything else you might want while in the park. I suggest visiting a grocery store and picking up snack foods and drinks for your time in the park. You will get better prices here than in the park itself. There are no chain grocery stores in the park.

Chapter 2

WHAT COULD A TYPICAL DAY AT YELLOWSTONE LOOK LIKE?

My ideal day at Yellowstone, or any national park for that matter, is built around hiking. Let me be clear though that there are many ways to enjoy Yellowstone, even if you do not wish to hike at all or are not physically up to it. However, allow me to describe my ideal day at Yellowstone, which is usually built around the park's fantastic hiking trails!

Numerous hikes can take you to see unbelievable natural beauty, including waterfalls, geysers, and wildlife, which you have probably seen numerous times on calendars and wondered where the pictures were taken. Day hiking offers solitude, backcountry beauty, impromptu wildlife sightings, exercise, and the opportunity to get away from the "obviously out of their element" visitor (remember the comment about my parents spending a whole two hours at Yellowstone?). Quality hikes also allow you to eat to your heart's content throughout your trip and still return home to stand on the scale and see that you actually lost weight on your vacation.

My family and I usually pick up breakfast items at one of the many grocery or snack stores within the park. Groceries are available at the General Stores at Canyon Village, Fishing Bridge, Grant Village, Lake, Mammoth, Tower, and Old Faithful (two locations, Lower and Upper General Stores), plus the Mini Store at Grant Village. All of these stores close for the winter season between early September and early October with the exception of the Mammoth General Store, which is open year-round. There is a more limited selection of snacks available at the Outdoor Stores located at Bridge Bay (closes early September) and Canyon Village (closes mid-October). My family and I once got ice cream cones at the Fishing Bridge General Store and just sat outside taking in the water, bridge, and surrounding beauty. It was one of those "priceless" memories that I will remember my entire life.

We usually pick up muffins, fruit, cereal, juice, and milk. This makes for a very economical breakfast, and more importantly, it is a big time saver. We can quickly eat while getting ready in our room, cabin, or tent, and hit the hiking trail much earlier than a formal restaurant breakfast will allow.

However, after breakfast, our next stop is for food again. Prior to hitting the trail, you must make sure you have more than enough food in your backpack (did I forget to mention that you will want to get a decent backpack?) to satisfy lunch and snacking while on the trail. While we are on the subject of backpacks, I STRONGLY suggest getting a CamelBak®, or one of its competitors, where the pack includes a bladder scientifically designed to keep the water ice cold. My family and I all hike with these. I once spent five hours in the Grand Canyon at around a hundred degrees, and when I finished my hike, I still had ice in my water. When you are thirsty or simply drinking regularly to keep yourself hydrated, there is a big difference in the quenched thirst factor between drinking ice-cold water and drinking warm water! It is well worth the expense. Backpacks of this type will cost you roughly $50 to $110.

I will tell you here that my favorite moments from any national park trip are the lunches on the trail. Don't knock it until you experience it! To find a flat rock to sit on and lay out your sub sandwich, chips, trail mix, etc. while enjoying a pristine view along the trail is as good as life gets! Anyway, you do not have to be a health freak when planning food for the backpack, just be sure you place a mix of items, including some that are healthy and provide quick energy. I always get a sub sandwich, fruit (apple, banana, or raisins), and a PowerBar®. However, I also might include a big cookie, Fig Newtons®, or potato chips; after all, you do want to enjoy yourself on vacation, right? Also, while you should pack at least 150 percent of as much food and water as you think you'll need, it also does not hurt to take along a soft drink. I usually drink only water while on the trail, but I enjoy a soft drink while stopped for lunch. Also, remember to take all your trash with you. This is what the signs mean that read, "Pack it in, pack it out."

Picking a trail isn't hard. However, picking the right trail is very important, for both your enjoyment and your safety. You do not want to hike beyond your limits. You can get hiking books on the entire park for a reasonable price at the visitor center bookstores, General Stores/souvenir shops, gift shops, at your local chain bookstore, or through the Internet. You can often find free hiking maps published for specific sections of the park through the Internet. Check out the official NPS Yellowstone Internet site for trail maps and descriptions at www.nps.gov/yell/planyourvisit/hiking. htm. There are often free individual trail handouts available from park rangers or visitor center counter personnel at the various visitor centers at Yellowstone, or you can purchase a "Day Hike Sampler" for just 50 cents at any visitor center bookstore. Also, be sure to get sage and up-to-the minute advice from a park ranger while visiting any visitor center. You will want to pick a trail that has the degree of difficulty that's appropriate, scenic offerings that appeal to you, and a time estimate that fits your time allocation. In other words, be smart. If you have never hiked before, start with an easy or moderate hike. Also, if the time estimate is say, four to six hours, start in the morning, not at 4:00 p.m. Be sure to be aware of and inquire about bear sightings. No need to panic here; just be sure to read chapter eleven!

Build your way up to tougher trails. You might try an easy trail on day one, a moderate trail on day two, take a break from hiking on day three, and then if you have yet to really push or challenge yourself, try a strenuous hike on day four.

Anyway, a day hike for me usually ends in mid to late afternoon. While hiking provides an unbelievably satisfying feeling of accomplishment for me, it leaves me more than ready to enjoy a hearty dinner, ranger lecture, and an early bedtime, because the next day, I begin the cycle once again.

Again, if you do not like to hike, are not physically up to hiking, or simply do not wish to hike, Yellowstone offers so many other options. There are geysers and other thermal features to see, fantastic hotels and lodges to explore, visitor centers with exhibits, movies, and knowledgeable personnel and park rangers to assist you, fishing, boating, bird watching, wildlife to watch that is second to none at any other park or place in the United States, and more. Chapter six goes into these options and many more in detail.

Chapter 3

WHERE WILL I SLEEP?

A nother great thing about Yellowstone is that accommodations are varied and sufficient in number, but only available if you plan ahead. National parks are not the type of place where you pull into town and start looking for the local Holiday Inn®. If you plan a year in advance or at least six to eight months, you will have a much more enjoyable park experience.

Within the park are varied types of accommodations ranging from a couple of hotels, to lodges, to modern cabins, to older and more rustic cabins. Some accommodations come with private bath while some provide shared bathroom and shower facilities. Some options are open only during the summer season while a couple are available for the summer season as well as the winter season. This is different from open year-round. There are no accommodations in Yellowstone National Park that are open 365 nights a year. The Mammoth Hot Springs Hotel and the Old Faithful Snow Lodge are open for the long summer season, then closed for a month or two before opening for an approximately three-month winter season, then closed for about a month before re-opening for another summer season. Specific dates and prices for winter 2010/2011, as well as the 2011 summer season are listed under each specific lodging option; all rates and dates are subject to change. While I list the dates for the current year as this book goes to press, these dates should not be viewed as quickly outdated information. The exact dates vary with each calendar year but should remain very similar, give or take just a few days for each subsequent year. They will give you a good idea of the park's seasons for any year, while you can call the park at the numbers listed below to get the exact dates for the year you plan to visit. Again, the earlier you plan, AND BOOK, your vacation the better. Any lodging prices mentioned in this book are for parties of two adults, do not include tax, and are current as of August 2010. Also, please note that all park accommodations are nonsmoking. All in-park lodging options are operated by Xanterra Parks & Resorts. Reservations can be made by calling Xanterra at 866-GEYSERLAND (866-439-7375) or 307-344-7311. Reservations can be made as of May 1 for any dates the following year.

Let me also say here that as you read the following options, please do not make the mistake of thinking it is best to pick your favorite option and book lodging there for your entire vacation at Yellowstone. This is far too massive a national park to plan to stay at just one location. You will want to plan each day's activities in such a way that allows you to travel through the park and have logically planned lodging to accommodate this movement. For example, if you plan a week at Yellowstone, you might plan to stay two nights at any of the Grant Village or Old Faithful area lodging options, then spend three nights at a place located in the center of the park, such as Canyon

Village, then spend the last two nights at Mammoth Hot Springs. You might also want to plan something similar to what I just suggested only in reverse and then move south out of the park to spend some time at Grand Teton National Park. Also, while there are many parks where I highly suggest spending every night in a cabin—such as the north rim of the Grand Canyon, Zion, or Isle Royale national parks, Yellowstone is a park where I prefer the lodges and hotels. This is not meant to suggest that I do not like the cabins; rather, it is a compliment to the very nice, historic, and numerous lodges and hotels such as those at Yellowstone Lake, Old Faithful, and Mammoth Hot Springs. At the same time, why not mix it up. I like to spend nights in lodges and hotels in the northern and southern parts of the park (Old Faithful and Mammoth Hot Springs) and spend a few nights in cabins in the Canyon Village or more central sections of Yellowstone. It is approximately a hundred-mile drive from the south entrance to the north entrance of this park, depending on the route you take. The roads in the heart of the park are laid out in a figure eight. If you plan your lodging at just one location, especially if it is at Grant Village or Mammoth Hot Springs, and plan to see all major sites in the park, you will be spending a lot of time driving and will learn the hard way that you did not properly plan your vacation. My wife and I once had a fantastic dinner at Mammoth Hot Springs, while still having to drive back to our lodging in the southern part of the park. As we dined, darkness fell and a severe thunderstorm came out of nowhere. We drove for nearly two hours in a driving thunderstorm, rarely seeing other cars, through the winding roads on what seemed like a never-ending drive to get back to our lodging. There are lakes to drive into, lots of wildlife roaming around, and plenty of darkness that you

9

do not want to force yourself into at the end of each day to return to poorly laid-out lodging reservations. Now let's talk specifics!

Old Faithful Inn

The **Old Faithful Inn** is one of the largest log structures in the world. Thankfully, due to the brave work of tremendously well-trained and dedicated firefighters, plus a little good fortune from Mother Nature, this structure still stands today (details in chapter fifteen: Wildfires). This is the most famous structure in Yellowstone National Park and is located in the most well-known section of the park—the geyser area. The lodge was built in 1904, has 329 rooms, and is known for its interior timber, three-story lobby, and massive stone fireplace. While I seldom promote just sitting around in a national park, I must admit that the best place to observe others (people watch) is in one of the comfortable chairs right in front of this unbelievably beautiful fireplace in the lobby of the Old Faithful Inn. The inn has undergone much renovation and features a gift shop and restaurant within the building, queen-size beds in most rooms, private refrigerators in the suites, and a large balcony porch available for any to use for a great view of "Old Faithful" geyser.

This lodging option features a wide variety of rooms ranging from suites with private bath, to premium rooms with private bath, to mid-range rooms with private baths, to basic rooms with shared bathrooms available down the hall. The Old Faithful Inn is open a long summer season (May 20—October 16, 2011), but closed in the winter (the Old Faithful Snow Lodge next door is open both summer and winter seasons). Radio, television, air conditioning, and Internet connections are intentionally not provided in order to provide the desired natural Yellowstone atmosphere. There are also numerous published articles claiming that this property is haunted. I have stayed in this great and historic facility and have never seen any signs of the supernatural; however, this rumor, in my opinion, just adds to the experience. Prices range from a high of $502 for a suite, to $96 for the basic rooms with shared bathroom facilities.

The **Old Faithful Snow Lodge & Cabins** comprise a large and much newer facility than the Old Faithful Inn; construction of its 134 units was completed in 1999. I have stayed in this facility as well. It was built to accommodate the great demand in this section of the park for more overnight accommodations than the Old Faithful Inn could handle by itself. Also, there was a desire for both summer and winter accommodations in this bitterly cold part of the country that the Old Faithful Inn—over a century old and very drafty—was not best prepared to satisfy. While there is nearly a century's difference in their age, Yellowstone National Park and the National Park Service, as they always do, did a fantastic job of building a brand new facility right next to one a century old that blend together very naturally and very nicely. Just as with the Old Faithful Inn, the Old Faithful Snow Lodge intentionally does not provide radio, television, air conditioning, or Internet connections, in order to preserve the desired natural Yellowstone atmosphere.

Available are "Lodge Rooms," with full bathrooms and telephones located in the rooms, and "Accessible Lodge Rooms," which look basically the same as the regular "Lodge Rooms" except that they have specially designed roll-in showers and accessible toilets and sinks. There are cabins called "Western Cabins," which are slightly older, as they were built in 1989. They sit in groups of four and provide two queen-size beds and a full bathroom. There are also "Accessible Western Cabins," which are very similar to the "Western Cabin" rooms but offer accessible bathtub with handrails, portable shower-hose attachments, and accessible toilet and sink. They have wheelchair entry ramps outside each unit. Most lodge rooms have double beds while the cabins feature queen-size beds.

The Old Faithful Snow Lodge Obsidian Dining Room and the Geyser Grill are located on the property. Again, the Old Faithful Snow Lodge is open for both a summer and a winter season. It is one of only two in-park lodging facilities open for a winter season. However, remember that this is not the same as being open year-round. There are dates where the lodge is closed. The lodge will be open for its 2010/2011 winter season from December 18, 2010, through March 7, 2011, while its 2011 summer season is scheduled from April 29 through October 23. Per night prices for lodging accommodations at the Old Faithful Snow Lodge range from $197 for a Lodge Room to $96 for a cabin. By the way, pets are allowed in the cabins.

Old Faithful Lodge Cabins represent the most economical way (other than camping) to stay in the most famous and busiest section of the park. This lodging option is comprised of ninety-six cabins plus a main lodge building completed in the 1920s. Amenities include a bakery, food court, gift store, post office, and general store. This is a summer season option scheduled to be open in 2011 from May 13 through September 25. There are Frontier Cabins with full private bathrooms, and Budget Cabins with communal showers located in the main lodge and toilets and sinks located near the cabins.

Prices range from $108 for a Frontier Cabin to $66 for a Budget Cabin. Pets are allowed in the cabins.

Grant Village is a very moderately priced option that is the most traditionally motel style of any in-park option. It was built in 1984, is comprised of three hundred rooms, and was named after President Ulysses S. Grant who signed the bill that established Yellowstone as the country's and the world's first national park in 1872. Grant Village is located on the southwest shore of Yellowstone Lake, is just twenty miles from the Old Faithful area, is the closest in-park lodging to Grand Teton National Park, and is close to one of the park's general stores and a gas station. This was the first place I stayed on my first trip to Yellowstone. This was in the late 1980s and I remember being very satisfied with the room I got considering this is one of the more moderately priced options in the park. If the other sites I have visited more recently are any gauge, I'm sure it is just as nice today as it was then.

Dinner options on the property are the Grant Village Dining Room and the Lake House; the Lake House provides excellent views of Yellowstone Lake. All rooms have private telephones and private bathrooms, complete with shower or shower/tub, toilet, and sink. There are ten handicapped accessible rooms all located on the ground floor providing roll-in showers and accessible toilets and sinks. Grant Village lodging is scheduled to be open for its 2011 season from May 27 through October 2. The price is $149 for a Hotel Room with Bath.

Lake Yellowstone Hotel

The **Lake Yellowstone Hotel and Cabins** is your most elegant lodging option in the park. The hotel is a massive eye-catching structure radiating memories of early twentieth-century class and attention to detail. The main hotel is the oldest operating hotel in the park, built in 1891, restored to its 1920s' atmosphere in 1990, and then remodeled in 2003/2004. The main hotel overlooks Yellowstone Lake and is painted in an eye-catching, yet classy yellow/golden color that really stands out against the pine forests surrounding the hotel. There are 196 guest rooms with many room type options from a Presidential Suite with two bedrooms, queen beds, and two full bathrooms, to premium rooms, high-range rooms, and handicapped-accessible rooms. The associated 110 cabins are less elegant and offer a much more economical way to stay on this site. Again, pets are allowed in the cabins only.

The Lake Yellowstone Hotel has the finest dining room in the park and the lobby offers live piano music nightly. The hotel is scheduled to be open for its 2011 season from May 13 through October 2. This location often sells out up to a year in advance so be sure to book as early as you can. Room rates range from $545 for the Presidential Suite to a range of $219 to $145 for regular lodge rooms to $130 for the Frontier Cabins.

The **Mammoth Hot Springs Hotel & Cabins** comprise the in-park lodging option just inside the north entrance to Yellowstone NP coming in from the Montana border. I have not stayed here, but I have had the pleasure of eating in its dining room multiple times. This area is a unique section of the park. The architecture is quite different from the more rustic style of the majority of Yellowstone. The Mammoth Hot Springs area is more like a small town than, say, the Old Faithful area. It is the most developed and town like with more formal streets with curbs, streetlights, and a feel of having reached a small town after driving many miles through very remote backcountry. This is not a negative; rather, it is a prime example of why you need to see all parts of this national park and see as many national parks as you can in your lifetime. If you have seen just one section of Yellowstone National Park, then you have seen just one section of the park! Also, the Mammoth Hot Springs Hotel is one of just two facilities (the Old Faithful Snow Lodge being the other) that is open for the winter season as well. Again, this does not mean the hotel is open year-round. It is closed just prior to and just after the winter season. The hotel expects to be open for what it calls its winter season from December 21, 2010, through March 7, 2011, while its 2011 summer season is scheduled from May 6 through October 10. This section of the park offers the Mammoth Hotel Dining Room, The Terrace Grill, a medical clinic, one of the park's general stores, a gas station, and much more.

The main lodge was completed in 1936 and offers 211 rooms for the summer season, and 100 available in winter. Options include just two suites that provide cable TV, two queen beds, and private bathrooms; midrange rooms with showers and double beds; and rooms with shared bathroom and shower facilities down the hall. (Note the trivia here. The just-mentioned two suites are the only lodging rooms in all of Yellowstone National Park that offer television!) There are Hot Tub Cabins with private hot tubs and bathrooms, to Frontier Cabins with private bathrooms, to Budget Cabins with shared bathrooms and showers located nearby.

Room rates range from $439 for a suite in summer or winter, to $117 for a room with private bath, to $87 for rooms with shared bathroom facilities. Cabins run from $213 for the Hot Tub Cabins to $109 for Frontier Cabins to $79 for Budget Cabins. Cabins are available for the summer season only and, like most cabins at Yellowstone, allow pets.

Lake Lodge Cabins Main Building

The **Lake Lodge Cabins** are yet another option within Yellowstone and like all options, is somewhat different than any other option. Not all of the 186 rooms/cabins are what you would envision as free-standing units. The units called Western Cabins are comprised of buildings with four to six connected units and are simply called cabins. I have stayed here, and there are pros and cons to choosing this option. The site is rather remote, located just off Yellowstone Lake, and, like most cabin options, offers much more solitude and national park get-away then any of the lodge or hotel options. The main lodge is a fantastic building with two large fireplaces, and plenty of tables to talk, play a game of cards, or just sit back and enjoy a good book. A gift shop, laundry facilities, and the Lake Lodge Cafeteria are available to you. The downside is that when I stayed here, it was not up to the same standards as the many other places I've stayed in the park. I do not mean that it was bad or a complete disaster. The units needed minor repairs and some housekeeping items were not up to the high standards that I had experienced elsewhere in the park. Some of these cabins were built in the 1920s and, to be fair, the park information on this facility states that some of the units have been recently remodeled.

Cabins are offered as Western Cabins for $166 a night, Frontier Cabins for $96, and 1920s-built Pioneer Cabins for $68. The 2011 summer season is expected to run from June 10 through September 25. Again, good news, these cabins also allow pets.

Canyon Lodge Cabins

The **Canyon Lodge & Cabins** are located right in the center of the park. This is a great location for visiting the Grand Canyon of Yellowstone and for many of the best hiking options. The Cascade Lodge building was built in 1992, the Dunraven Lodge building was completed in 1998, while the cabins were constructed in the 1950s and 1960s. The Old Faithful Inn and the Lake Yellowstone Hotel are magnificent, and I most highly recommend these accommodations. However, if you are considering one of the cabin offerings, I really like the Canyon Cabins (the Western Cabins were recently refurbished). Again, the location is central, the cabins are well maintained, the property is heavily wooded, and, at least when I stayed here just after we welcomed the new millennium, I got bear-shaped bars of soap. I still have a few of these and they represent one of the best souvenirs of the trip. On-site offerings include the Canyon Lodge Dining Room, a cafeteria, deli, laundry facilities, and a gift shop.

There are over 480 lodging units, designed in three room types, all are motel style with full private baths, and are reasonably priced. Open only for the summer season, as are all cabins at Yellowstone, the Canyon Lodge and Cabins expects to be open for the 2011 season from June 3 through September 5 (Western Cabins available through 9/25). Prices range from $166 for a lodge room or Western Cabin, to $96 for a Frontier Cabin, to $70 for a Pioneer Cabin. Again, pets are allowed in cabins.

Roosevelt Lodge Cabins are named after President Theodore Roosevelt in remembrance of his love for this northeastern area of the park. There are eighty units, a general store, a gift shop, a gas station, and the Roosevelt Lodge Dining Room. The Lodge Dining Room hosts Old West Dinner Cookouts accessible only by choosing to take a horseback ride or covered wagon ride to get you to the site.

Cabins come in two types; the Frontier Cabins with double beds and full private bath, and the Roughrider Cabins heated with wood-burning stoves and shared showers and bathrooms located nearby. The 2011 season for this lodging option is June 10 through September 5 and prices are $108 for a Frontier Cabin and $65 for a Roughrider Cabin. Roosevelt Lodge Cabins are the only cabins in the entire park that DO NOT allow pets. I called the park and verified this, although the person who confirmed this was not sure of the reason why.

I will add TWO BIG PIECES OF ADVICE here. One: book early, six months to a year in advance if you can. Two: if you book on short notice and cannot get the overnight accommodations you desire, do not give up, call back regularly. My wife, on one of our trips to Yosemite NP, at the encouragement of the reservation desk, simply called every evening to inquire about cancellations. I must add that the reservation folks were very friendly and more than willing to take her call every night. At approximately two weeks out, as it is common for lots of people to cancel, we ended up getting four nights in one location and two nights at another location in the park—just what we wanted in the first place. If you are persistent, it may pay off. Yellowstone NP accepts reservations for the summer season beginning May 1 of the preceding year, and March 15 for the following winter season.

To summarize, park lodging consists of the following number of units:

Old Faithful Inn	329 rooms
Old Faithful Snow Lodge & Cabins	134 units
Old Faithful Lodge Cabins	96 cabins
Grant Village	300 rooms
Lake Yellowstone Hotel	196 rooms
Lake Yellowstone Hotel Cabins	110 cabins
Mammoth Hot Springs Hotel/Cabins	211 rooms (summer) 100 rooms (winter)
Lake Lodge Cabins	186 units
Canyon Lodge & Cabins	480 units
Roosevelt Lodge Cabins	80 units

Finally, there are twelve campgrounds within the park boundaries of Yellowstone. Seven are first-come, first-served, and cannot be reserved in advance. The National Park Service operates these sites, which are $12 to $14 a night and are all seasonal locations open from either May or June through September or October. These sites are:

Norris
Indian Creek
Pebble Creek
Tower Fall
Slough Creek
Louis Lake
Mammoth*

*Mammoth is the only site available year-round.

There are five campgrounds operated by Xanterra Parks & Resorts (the same company that operates all the lodges and cabins within the park boundaries). Reservations can be made by calling toll-free in advance 866-GEYSERLAND (866-439-7375) or on the same day as requested by calling 307-344-7311. These sites are all $19.50 with the exception of Fishing Bridge. This is a hard-sided RV-only park with a nightly charge of $28.00. Campground reservations, again for those that operate on a reservation-based system, are accepted beginning May 1 for the summer season of the following year. This is basically twelve to sixteen months in advance. These sites are:

Bridge Bay**
Canyon**
Grant Village**
Madison**
Fishing Bridge RV

** Handicapped-accessible sites available

Fishing Bridge RV Park is the only site with water, sewer, and electrical hookups and is for hard-sided RVs only. This is the only site within the park boundary for large RVs (over thirty feet); therefore, early reservations are strongly suggested. If you have a large RV and this site has no vacancy, there are locations outside the park boundaries for large RVs at Flagg Ranch, Gardiner, and West Yellowstone.

There are also numerous hotel, motel, and cabin accommodations located just outside the park, most of these in West Yellowstone. They are the predictable chain and local motel options. They are fine, many very new, and they are often cheaper than any of the fine lodges located in the park. However, if you can afford to spend just a little more, the lodges and hotels in Yellowstone National Park are fantastic, historic, and will greatly enhance your park experience. Not only are the locations in the park much better for limiting your time in the car (you spend enough time in the car at home, right?), but they offer fantastic memorable experiences that you will cherish your entire life. I'LL STATE IT EMPHATICALLY, RIGHT HERE, THAT THE PARK EXPERIENCE IS BEST IF YOU STAY RIGHT IN THE PARK! To wake up and step outside to see geysers, wildlife, or hot springs right in front of you, beats the heck out of stepping out of a chain motel you have back home to see a fast food establishment across the parking lot. Having said this, I find the towns located just outside the park boundaries to be delightful and charming, but they are not Yellowstone National Park. You've come so far—get inside the park!

I strongly recommend requesting information on Yellowstone directly from the park. The park can be contacted at 307-344-7381 or via their Web site at www. nps.gov/yell. You can obtain information on lodging, camping, road conditions, weather, fees, backcountry use, employment, and much more.

I have listed the phone numbers and Web sites in chapter nine for the local Chamber of Commerce offices, serving the surrounding towns of West Yellowstone, Gardiner, Silver Gate, and Cooke City, Montana; Cody, Wyoming; and more to assist in your trip planning.

Again, please note that you WILL NOT find the usual chain hotels (thanks goodness). The accommodations just outside the park, for the most part, are very quaint, clean, and possess much more character than the chains you are used to in the more typical vacation hot spots (Orlando for example). Most are great and very nice. They simply are not in as good a location as accommodations within the park boundaries.

Chapter 4

WHERE WILL I EAT?

Yellowstone NP offers a surprising number of options for mealtime. Casual and economical dining is available at one of the many cafeterias available at the Old Faithful Lodge, the Lake Lodge, or the Canyon Lodge, where you can get a surprisingly good meal for the price you'd expect at a cafeteria. Or select fine dining at any of the lodges or hotels with more options than you will probably find back home.

While stating that there are many options, and there really are, you will find seven dinner options (six locations with two options at Old Faithful) at the various main stops throughout the park. All the dining room menus have variety and numerous options, yet are very similar to each other. This is intentional, as the logical way to have a nice dinner is to make a reservation at the location closest to where you are spending that particular night lodging in the park. If you know your plans, and I highly advise thoroughly planning out each day at Yellowstone prior to your arrival, I suggest making dinner reservations (where accepted or required) through the front desk where you are lodging as soon as you arrive, if not prior to your arrival. It is hard to know where you want to eat each night prior to arriving at the park; however, if you wait to make reservations until you arrive, you may be forced to eat very early or very late in the evening. Don't expect to walk up and make a reservation for the same day at 5:30 or 6:00 p.m.! You must call Xanterra at 1-866-GEYSERLAND (866-439-7375) or 307-344-7311 or book dinner reservations in person; they cannot be booked through the Web site. Breakfast and lunch are first-come, first-seated throughout the park. Please note that any prices mentioned in this book are as of August 2010. Dates, select prices, and hours of operation are identified as 2010 or 2011 based upon the most current information available. I elected to include these, not to quickly date information in this book, but because hopefully it is very useful at **providing "ballpark" information that will only change very slightly from one year to another.** By the way, I have made every attempt to confirm hours and dates listed; however, they change quite often, can vary from one internet source to another, and sometimes even differ from a Web site to the same sites listed phone contact if you call. I strongly advise confirming service hours upon arrival!

The fanciest dining room in the entire park is the Lake Hotel Dining Room (inside the Lake Yellowstone Hotel). This is the park's oldest and most elegant hotel and thus its most elegant dining as well. This is probably the only place you might feel out of place in casual vacation wear. They probably will not turn you away if you show up in jeans and a Yellowstone T-shirt, but you might want to pack a collared shirt and slacks for the dining room here. The dinner menu here is slightly more expensive than the other hotel dining rooms. It also offers a fabulous view of Yellowstone Lake. Selections include beef tenderloin,

Alaskan halibut, duck breast, and surf and turf. Main course prices range from $13.95 to $36.00. Quicker, less expensive and less formal food such as soup, sandwiches, and snacks are available at both the Lake Hotel Deli and the nearby Lake Lodge Cafeteria.

Lake Yellowstone Hotel Dining Room
2010 dates and hours of operation:
May 21 through September 26
Breakfast: 6:30 a.m. – 10:00 a.m.
Lunch: 11:30 a.m. – 2:30 p.m.
Dinner 5:00 p.m. – 10:00 p.m.
Dress Code: casual
Reservations: recommended for dinner

Lake Hotel Deli
2010 dates and hours of operation:
May 21 through September 25
Coffee and Breakfast Pastries: 6:30 a.m. – 10:30 a.m. (May 27 – September 6)
Sandwiches to order: 10:30 a.m. – 8:00 p.m. (May 21 – May 26)
Sandwiches to order: 10:30 a.m. – 9:00 p.m. (May 27 – August 4)
Sandwiches to order: 10:30 a.m. – 8:30 p.m. (August 5 – September 6)
Sandwiches to order: 2:30 p.m. – 8:00 p.m. (September 7 – September 25)
Dress Code: casual
Reservations: not accepted

Lake Lodge Cafeteria
2010 dates and hours of operation:
June 10 through October 2
Breakfast: 6:30 a.m. – 10:00 a.m. (June 10 – September 6)

Breakfast: 7:00 a.m. – 10:00 a.m. (September 7 – October 2)

Continental Breakfast: 6:30 a.m. – 11:30 a.m. (June 10 – September 6)

Continental Breakfast: 7:00 a.m. – 10:30 a.m. (September 7 – October 2)

Lunch: 11:30 a.m. – 2:30 p.m. (June 10 – September 6)

Lunch: 12:00 noon – 3:00 p.m. (September 7 – October 2)

Dinner: 4:30 p.m. – 10:00 p.m. (June 10 – September 6)

Dinner: 5:00 p.m. – 9:00 p.m. (September 7 – October 2)

Dress Code: casual

Reservations: not accepted

The Mammoth Hotel Dining Room (located at the Mammoth Hot Springs Hotel) offers just a slight step down in fanciness, is located on the parade grounds of the original Fort Yellowstone, and regularly provides great views of wandering elk and bison while you enjoy your dining experience. This is also one of just a couple of locations in Yellowstone NP (the other being The Old Faithful Snow Lodge) offering both summer and winter operating dates. Main course features include prime rib, bison, trout, and lamb linguini. There are also lighter fare choices for those not as hungry, soups and salads. Main courses range from $10.95 to $23.95. Quicker, less expensive, and less formal food including sandwiches, salads, and ice cream are available at the Mammoth Terrace Grill.

Mammoth Hotel Dining Room

2010 dates and hours of operation:

May 14 through October 11 and December 21, 2010 through breakfast on March 8, 2011

Breakfast: 6:30 a.m. – 10:00 a.m.

Breakfast Buffet (Sundays and Mondays in winter season only): 6:30 a.m. – 10:30 a.m.

28

Lunch: 11:30 a.m. – 2:30 p.m.

Dinner: 5:00 p.m. – 10:00 p.m. (5:30 p.m. – 8:00 p.m. winter season)

Dress Code: casual

Reservations: recommended for dinner, winter season only

Mammoth Terrace Grill

2010 dates of operation:

April 30 through October 17

Breakfast: 8:00 a.m. – 10:30 a.m. (June 10 – June 23)

Breakfast: 7:30 a.m. – 10:30 a.m. (June 24 – September 8)

Breakfast: 8:00 a.m. – 10:30 a.m. (September 9 – September 15)

Continental Breakfast: 8:30 a.m. – 11:00 a.m. (April 30 – June 9)

Continental Breakfast: 8:00 a.m. – 11:00 a.m. (June 10 – June 23)

Continental Breakfast: 7:30 a.m. – 11:00 a.m. (June 24 – September 8)

Continental Breakfast: 8:00 a.m. – 11:00 a.m. (September 9 – October 11)

Lunch/Dinner: 11:00 a.m. – 5:30 p.m. (April 30 – May 14)

Lunch/Dinner: 11:00 a.m. – 7:00 p.m. (May 15 – June 9)

Lunch/Dinner: 11:00 a.m. – 8:00 p.m. (June 10 – June 23)

Lunch/Dinner: 11:00 a.m. – 9:00 p.m. (June 24 – September 8)

Lunch/Dinner: 11:00 a.m. – 8:00 p.m. (September 9 – September 15)

Lunch/Dinner: 11:00 a.m. – 7:00 p.m. (September 16 – October 11)

Lunch/Dinner: 11:00 a.m. – 5:00 p.m. (October 12 – October 17)

Ice Cream: 11:00 a.m. – 5:30 p.m. (April 30 – May 14)

Ice Cream: 11:00 a.m. – 7:00 p.m. (May 15 – June 9)

Ice Cream: 11:00 a.m. – 8:00 p.m. (June 10 – June 23)
Ice Cream: 11:00 a.m. – 9:00 p.m. (June 24 – September 8)
Ice Cream: 11:00 a.m. – 8:00 p.m. (September 9 – September 15)
Ice Cream: 11:00 a.m. – 7:00 p.m. (September 16 – October 11)
Ice Cream: 11:00 a.m. – 5:00 p.m. (October 12 – October 17)
Dress Code: casual
Reservations: not accepted

The geyser area is obviously one of the most populated areas of the park and for this reason, offers multiple dining options. The Old Faithful Inn (an absolute MUST-SEE itself) offers both a dining room and the Bear Paw Deli; located right next door is the Old Faithful Snow Lodge Obsidian Dining Room. The Old Faithful Inn dining room offers its signature dinner buffet, which offers prime rib of beef, Caesar salad, chicken wings, green beans amandine, baked beans, baked potatoes, Italian mushrooms, red pepper with smoked gouda soup, and rolls. The buffet price is $23.75 for adults and $10.95 for kids. You can also order off the menu for items that include rib eye steak, chicken, salmon, bison burger, bison ravioli, swordfish, and trout. Prices range from $9.95 to $29.95. Besides the dining room and the Bear Claw Deli, other food and beverage options at the Old Faithful Inn include the Old Faithful Lodge Cafeteria and Bake Shop and the second floor mezzanine espresso cart and bar. The Old Faithful Lodge Cafeteria & Bake Shop offers hot entrees, salads, sandwiches, and pastas. The bake shop offers baked goods as well as deli sandwiches.

Located right next door and only a short walk from the historic Old Faithful Inn is The Old Faithful Snow Lodge offering the Obsidian Dining Room, the Geyser Grill, and the Firehole Lounge. The dining room menu features selections including prime rib, salmon, and chicken. The menu here is more limited than those previously discussed and main course prices range from $15.00 for the burger to $29.95 for the wild boar tenderloin. They also offer chicken, salmon, and a few other selections. The Obsidian Dining Room is one of only two dining rooms (the other being the Mammoth Hotel Dining Room) that is open for business during the winter season as well. As is becoming a theme here, lighter and cheaper fare can be obtained at the Geyser Grill including burgers, deli sandwiches, and salads.

Old Faithful Inn Dining Room
2010 dates and hours of operation:
May 7 through October 17
Breakfast: 6:30 a.m. – 10:00 a.m.
Breakfast Buffet and Continental Breakfast: 6:30 a.m. – 10:30 a.m.
Lunch: 11:30 a.m. – 2:30 p.m.
Dinner: 5:00 p.m. – 10:00 p.m. (May 7 – June 9, September 7 – October 17)
Dinner: 4:30 p.m. – 10:00 p.m. (June 10 – September 6)
Dress Code: casual
Reservations: recommended for dinner

The Bear Paw Deli (lunch, dinner, ice cream)
2010 dates and hours of operation:
May 7 through May 19/10:30 a.m. – 7:00 p.m.
May 20 through September 6/10:30 a.m. – 9:00 p.m.
September 7 through October 16/11:00 a.m. – 8:00 p.m.
Dress Code: casual
Reservations: not accepted

Old Faithful Lodge Cafeteria

2010 dates and hours of operation:
May 14 through September 25
Lunch: 11:00 a.m. – 4:30 p.m.
Dinner 4:30 p.m. – 9:00 p.m.
Dress Code: casual
Reservations: not accepted

Old Faithful Lodge Bake Shop

2010 dates and hours of operation:
May 14 through September 6, September 26 – 30/6:30 a.m. –
    10:00 p.m.
September 7 through September 25/6:30 a.m. – 8:00 p.m.
Dress Code: casual

Old Faithful Lodge Ice Cream Shop

2010 dates and hours of operation:
May 14 through May 21/11:00 a.m. – 9:00 p.m.
May 22 through September 6/10:00 a.m. – 9:00 p.m.
September 7 through September 30/11:00 a.m. – 7:00 p.m.
Dress Code: casual

Old Faithful Snow Lodge Obsidian Dining Room

2010 dates and hours of operation:
Summer, April 30 through October 24
Breakfast: 6:30 a.m. – 10:30 a.m.
Breakfast Buffet: 6:30 a.m. – 10:30 a.m.
Dinner: 5:00 p.m. – 10:00 p.m.

Winter, December 18, 2010 through breakfast on March 8, 2011
Breakfast: 6:30 a.m. – 10:00 a.m.
Lunch: 11:30 a.m. – 3:00 p.m.
Dinner: 5:00 p.m. – 9:30 p.m.

Dress Code: casual

Reservations: accepted for winter season dinner only

Old Faithful Snow Lodge Geyser Grill

Summer 2010 dates and hours of operation:

Breakfast: 8:00 a.m. – 10:30 a.m. (June 10 – August 25)

Continental Breakfast: 8:30 a.m. – 11:00 a.m. (May 15 – June 9)

Continental Breakfast: 8:00 a.m. – 11:00 a.m. (June 10 – August 25)

Lunch/Dinner: 11:00 a.m. – 5:00 p.m. (April 16 – May 14)

Lunch/Dinner: 11:00 a.m. – 7:00 p.m. (May 15 – June 9)

Lunch/Dinner: 11:00 a.m. – 9:00 p.m. (June 10 – August 25)

Lunch/Dinner: 10:30 a.m. – 7:00 p.m. (August 26 – October 16)

Lunch/Dinner: 11:00 a.m. – 5:00 p.m. (October 17 – November 7)

Winter 2010/2011 dates and hours of operation

Lunch and Dinner only

December 18, 2010 through March 6, 2011/10:30 a.m. – 5:00 p.m. guaranteed, hours may be extended.

Dress Code: casual

Reservations: not accepted

While visiting the Grant Village area, dining options are the Grant Village Dining Room and the Grant Village Lake House. Grant Village is the closest development to the south entrance as well as Grand Teton National Park and is only about a thirty-minute drive from the Geyser area featuring Old Faithful. This is a very wooded and beautiful area. The restaurant overlooks Yellowstone Lake and features a breakfast buffet. Dining room menu selections include multiple salads and a burger to main course options such as prime rib, bison top sirloin, bison meatloaf, pork chops, fish and chips, and the almost always available salmon option. Main course prices range from $9.95 to $23.95.

The Grant Village Lake House is located at the lake's edge and offers a breakfast buffet as well as a pub-style dinner menu featuring a selection of burgers, including beef, bison, chicken, and black bean. However, it is not open for lunch.

Grant Village Dining Room
2010 dates and hours of operation:
May 28 through October 3
Breakfast/Breakfast Buffet: 6:30 a.m. – 10:00 a.m.
Lunch: 11:30 a.m. – 2:30 p.m.
Dinner: 5:00 p.m. – 10:00 p.m.
Dress Code: casual
Reservations: required for dinner

Grant Village Lake House
2010 dates and hours of operation:
June 18 through September 25
Breakfast: 6:30 a.m. – 10:30 a.m.
Dinner: 5:00 p.m. – 9:30 p.m. (June 18 – June 30)
Dinner: 5:00 p.m. – 10:30 p.m. (July 1 – September 6)
Dinner: 5:00 p.m. – 9:00 p.m. (September 7 – September 25)
Dress Code: casual
Reservations: not accepted

The Roosevelt Lodge (located near Tower Fall just south of Tower Junction) features the Roosevelt Lodge Dining Room. This is the most rustic lodge with a very old west décor. The menu here features such unique offerings as barbeque ribs, elk, and catfish. As you might have guessed, you can also order fried chicken or trout. Prices range from $15.95 to $23.95.

Also offered are Old West Dinner Cookouts. These feature western entertainment, generous portions, steak (12 oz. adult, 6 oz. children), potato salad, the obligatory baked beans, corn, corn muffins, fruit crisp, watermelon, and assorted beverages. The cookouts are accessible only via horseback or covered wagon. The price for the Old West Dinner Cookout with covered wagon transportation is $55 adult, $45 children three to eleven years of age, children two and under free. The price with a one-hour horseback ride to the cookout is $66 adult, $56 children eight to eleven years of age. The price with the two-hour horseback ride to the cookout is $80 adult, $70 children eight to eleven years of age. Children under the age of eight must take the covered wagon option as they are not allowed to take either horseback ride option to the Old West Dinner Cookouts.

Roosevelt Lodge Dining Room
2010 dates and hours of operation:
June 11 through September 6
Breakfast: 7:00 a.m. – 10:00 a.m.
Lunch: 11:30 a.m. – 3:00 p.m.
Dinner: 4:30 p.m. – 9:00 p.m.
Dress Code: casual
Reservations: not accepted

Old West Dinner Cookouts
2010 dates and hours of operation:
June 12 through September 5
Check-in for one-hour horseback ride is 4:30 p.m. (3:30 p.m. as of mid-August)
Check-in for two-hour horseback ride is 3:45 p.m. (2:45 p.m. as of mid-August)

Check-in for covered wagon ride is 4:45 p.m. (3:45 p.m. as of mid-August)
Dress Code: casual
Reservations: required

In the Canyon Village area, dining is offered at the Canyon Lodge Dining Room, Cafeteria & Deli. The dining room is the least expensive of all the dining rooms in the park. Main course selections include fish and chips, beef burger, bison steak, pork chop, and, you guessed it, trout and prime rib. Main course prices range from $10.95 to $16.95 with the exception of the prime rib, which ranges from $16.95 to $23.95, depending on portion size. The dining room also offers a lunch buffet and a full dinner salad bar.

Canyon Lodge Dining Room
2010 dates and hours of operation:
June 4 through September 26
Breakfast Buffet: 7:00 a.m. – 10:00 a.m.
Lunch Buffet: 11:30 a.m. – 2:30 p.m.
Dinner: 5:00 p.m. – 10:00 p.m.
Dress Code: casual
Reservations: not accepted

Canyon Lodge Cafeteria
2010 dates and hours of operation:
June 4 through September 6
Breakfast: 6:30 a.m. – 11:00 a.m.
Lunch/Dinner: 11:30 a.m. – 9:30 p.m.
Dress Code: casual
Reservations: not accepted

Canyon Lodge Deli (snacks, beverages, deli sandwiches, and ice cream)
2010 dates and hours of operation:
June 4 through August 11/11:00 a.m. – 9:30 p.m.
August 12 through August 25/11:00 a.m. – 7:00 p.m.
August 26 through September 19/11:00 a.m. – 6:00 p.m.
Reservations: not accepted

In addition to regular dining venues and hours of operation, both the Mammoth Hot Springs Hotel and the Old Faithful Snow Lodge offer special dining events. Special events at the Mammoth Hot Springs Hotel include Sunday Breakfast Buffet, Christmas Day Dinner Buffet, New Year's Eve Dinner, a Specialty Chocolate Buffet (offered January 14 for 2011), a Brew Masters Dinner (offered January 21 for 2011), a Wine Tasting with upscale snacks and finger foods referred to as Tapas (offered January 28 for 2011), a Valentine's Day Dinner, and an International Market (offered February 18 for 2011).

The Old Faithful Snow Lodge special dining events are Christmas Day Dinner, New Year's Eve Dinner, a Brew Masters Dinner (offered January 14 for 2011), a Valentine's Day Dinner, and a Rocky Mountain Tapas (offered February 12 for 2011). Reservations are required for all special dining events at both the Mammoth Hot Springs Hotel and the Old Faithful Snow Lodge except for the International Market event.

Park publications sometimes refer to dinner reservations as "required," sometimes as "recommended," and sometimes as "accepted." To ensure that you have the best park experience possible, I suggest considering them as "required." Dinner reservations can be made for any of the locations just discussed and identified as requiring dinner reservations by calling 1-866 GEYSERLAND (866-439-7375) or 307-344-7311. Dining reservations are generally accepted beginning May 1 for any date the following year if you have lodging reservations at the same facility, or sixty days in advance without a room reservation. As you can see, with proper planning, you will not go hungry or be forced to eat an unhealthy diet at Yellowstone NP. If you just remember to plan ahead, make dinner reservations, know that only The Mammoth Hotel and the Old Faithful Snow Lodge offer winter hours of operation, dining can be a real highlight of your vacation at Yellowstone National Park.

Chapter 5

HIKING OPTIONS

While there are endless numbers of trails—far too many to list all of them—allow me to describe some of the best day hikes grouped by park area. First a few words of advice. Maybe you are a seasoned national park visitor or someone who at least gets out regularly into western wilderness. If so, you probably know what to watch out for and how to "hike smart." However, and I certainly mean no insult here, if you have never done any real hiking and are thinking Yellowstone would be a good place to start, please be sure to read on and take this activity seriously. I do not mean to scare anyone. Certainly you are very safe if you are just planning on short hikes from parking areas to view well known geysers via short boardwalk trails. However, the longest trails into the backcountry pose multiple threats: large wildlife, unpredictable weather, dangerous and ever-changing thermal areas, rugged rock, elevation change and its physical demands, active and very cold or boiling water temperatures, and areas where you will not have any cell phone coverage. In other words, know all the risks that come with heading from heavily populated areas into remote areas where, if you have a problem, you may be dependent on yourself and your survival skills to get out of it. Having said this, I am not trying to discourage hiking. Quite the opposite, it is my favorite activity at Yellowstone or any national park and is probably much safer then walking down the street in any major city; I just want to make sure you know what you are getting into. As I will always remember a park ranger at Jasper National Park in Alberta, Canada, telling me: there have been more people killed there by falling trees than by bears.

Talk to a park ranger before you hike any trail at Yellowstone longer than the short boardwalk trails to see famous geysers, or any trail into remote areas where you will spend much of your time out of site of other people. Even if you have done the trail before, conditions change. There may be more thermal activity or greater wildlife activity than the last time you were there. Be sure to be prepared with proper attire, sufficient amounts of food and water, and safety equipment including a first aid kit, a bear bell, and bear spray. When hiking in bear country, always make noise, talk to others, talk to yourself, sing, and yell "hello, bear." I always hike with a "bear bell" although there is some research claiming that these are not very helpful. Do not hike after dark and always hike with at least one other person. Yellowstone park regulations require you to stay at least one hundred yards from bears and wolves, twenty-five yards from all other wildlife including bison. Also, bear spray is not the same as the pepper spray you may have or be familiar with. The typical pepper spray (often referred to as mace), which is highly effective on humans, will not be effective against an attacking bear! More on this in chapter eleven.

The hikes in this chapter are listed by area of the park, and from shortest distance to longest distance within each section. The estimated times are very generous and are, for the most part, based upon official U.S. National Park Service publication estimates. If you are a regular walker, one who has hiked other national parks, or just a person who considers him or herself to be in pretty good shape, you can expect to complete the hikes in approximately two-thirds of the time estimated. That is, unless you spend lots of time stopped and just relaxing at some point along the trail. I strongly suggest purchasing a good hiking book; one full of easy to read trail maps and descriptions. They can be life-savers, or at least vacation-savers in helping to make sure you pick hikes appropriate for your abilities; they make great souvenirs as well. Another economical option is to purchase a "Day Hike Sampler" for just 50 cents at any visitor center bookstore.

DAY HIKES in the BAY BRIDGE, LAKE, and FISHING BRIDGE AREA

Pelican Creek (easy/1.3 miles/30–60 minutes)
This short hike gives one a taste of the area. You'll see forest, lakeshore, and marsh and it is a good spot for bird-watching. The trailhead is located west of the Pelican Creek Bridge, one mile east of the Fishing Bridge Visitor Center.

Elephant Back Mountain (moderate/3.6 miles/1.5–2.5 hours)
This hike provides up-close exposure to a dense lodgepole forest. It is a looping trail that intersects at

an overlook view of Yellowstone Lake. Be prepared for eight hundred feet of elevation change. The trailhead is located at a pullout one mile south of Fishing Bridge Junction.

Avalanche Peak (extremely strenuous/4.0 miles/3–4 hours)

This trail is a high elevation trail through known grizzly bear habitat. Again, make noise, travel with at least one other person, and carry bear spray. This hike will take you up twenty-one hundred feet in two miles, includes many switchbacks, and the crossing of a narrow ridgeline. Be careful, be smart, and be rewarded with excellent views of some of the park's highest and most remote mountain peaks. While you are always advised to check with a park ranger for updates on any trail, this one in particular should not be taken without asking at the Fishing Bridge Visitor Center for updates on weather, wildlife, and trail conditions! The trailhead is located nineteen miles east of Fishing Bridge junction or eight miles west of the East Entrance, across the road from the pullout at the west end of Eleanor Lake

Storm Point (easy/2.3 miles/1–2 hours)

Hopefully, this hike provides an excellent opportunity to see numerous yellow-bellied marmots. After walking through open meadows with views of Indian Pond and Yellowstone Lake, the trail enters forestland. After emerging from the trees, you will arrive at Storm Point, a rocky outcrop that is home to a large colony of marmots. Another hike in known bear country, this trail is sometimes closed in late spring and early summer due to bear activity. Be sure to inquire about closure at the Fishing Bridge Visitor Center. The trailhead is located at the Indian Pond pullout, three miles east of the Fishing Bridge Visitor Center.

Pelican Valley (moderately easy/6.8 miles/4–5 hours)
This trail takes you through some of the most grizzly bear-inhabited turf in the continental United States. Again, make noise, pay attention, and stay alert, do not hike alone, and be sure to carry bear spray. This very scenic hike travels through meadow and then forest. You'll cross several bridges and go through a small thermal area (stay on the trail here). There are excellent views of meadows, Pelican Creek, and the Absaroka Mountains to the east. The trail ends at the site of a washed-out bridge. Return is via the same route. The trailhead and parking can be found at the end of the gravel road across from Indian Pond, three miles east of the Fishing Bridge Visitor Center.

Howard Eaton (easy/7.0 miles/2.5–3.5 hours)
Starting on the east side of Fishing Bridge, this trail follows along the Yellowstone River for a short time, then ventures alongside the service road. You then travel through meadow and forest for views of the river. The last mile travels through dense lodgepole forests before ascending to an overlook of LeHardys Rapids. This is the end of the trail and you will need to return via the same route. There is an extension of this hike that continues to the Canyon area via a twelve-mile, not well maintained trail that would require a very early start, a full-day commitment, and an arranged vehicle pickup at the other

end. The trailhead is located at the parking lot on the east side of the Fishing Bridge.

DAY HIKES in the CANYON AREA

Mount Washburn (strenuous/2.5 or 3.1 miles/3–6 hours)

There are actually two trails and two trailhead options to hike to Mount Washburn. Both offer great views and an excellent chance to see bighorn sheep. Avoid this trail, and specifically the top of Mount Washburn, in storms and, in particular, when thunder can be heard in the area. Trailheads are located at Dunraven Pass, 4.5 miles north of Canyon Junction (3.1-mile hike one-way), and at Crittenden Road, 10.3 miles north of Canyon Junction (2.5-mile hike one-way).

Howard Eaton (easy/2.5-12.0 miles/3–8 hours)

This relatively easy trail travels through various parts of Yellowstone (as seen under Fishing Bridge trails) and allows you to hike varying distances based upon your preferences, available time, and hiking ability. This trail takes hikers through marsh, meadow, and forests and is 2.5 miles to Cascade Lake, 4.25 miles to Grebe Lake, 6.25 miles to Wolf Lake, 8.25 miles to Ice Lake, and 12.0 miles to the Norris Campground. The trailhead can be found at the pullout .25 mile west of Canyon Junction on the Norris–Canyon Road.

Cascade Lake (easy/5.0 miles/3 hours)

This is a great choice for the novice hiker, those not as young as they used to be, or those with limited time for hiking. This easy stroll is basically a walk through a beautiful meadow with wildflowers and the ever-present opportunity for wildlife watching. There are two trailhead options: a pullout located .25 miles west of Canyon Junction on the Norris–Canyon Road or the Cascade Lake Trailhead, 1.25 miles north of Canyon Junction on the Tower–Canyon Road.

Grebe Lake (moderately easy/6.0 miles/3–4 hours)
This trail travels along an old fire road through both forest and meadow including up-close views of sites burned in the historic fires of 1988. You'll have the option of connecting to the Howard Eaton Trail at Grebe Lake. The trailhead is located 3.5 miles west of Canyon Junction on the Norris–Canyon Road.

Observation Peak (strenuous/11.0 miles/7 hours)
This is an extension of the Cascade Lake Trail previously described leading to a high elevation for excellent views of the Yellowstone backcountry wilderness. You will enjoy pine forests and climb over fourteen hundred feet. The trailhead is the Cascade Lake Trailhead located 1.25 miles north of Canyon Junction on the Tower–Canyon Road.

Seven Mile Hole (strenuous/11.0 miles/6–8 hours)
This trail begins along the canyon rim and provides views of Silver Cord Cascade. It then joins the Washburn Spur Trail for three miles, bringing the hiker to the Seven Mile Hole. Be prepared for over one thousand feet of descent in this section. Be very careful and be sure to stay on the trail as it passes through both active and dormant hot springs.

Washburn Spur Trail (strenuous/11.0-11.5 miles/6–8 hours)
This is a spur trail heading east once you reach the top of Mount Washburn. The trail offers a very steep descent over rough terrain for 3.7 miles to Washburn Hot Springs. From this point you continue south (pass and do not take the turnoff for Seven Mile Hole) and end at the Glacial Boulder pullout on the road to Inspiration Point. Note: this trail passes through thermal areas and park authorities strongly advise staying on the marked trail. The Trailheads are the same trailheads previously described for Mount Washburn. Trailheads are located at Dunraven Pass, 4.5 miles north of Canyon Junction (a 3.1 mile hike one-way) and at Crittenden Road, 10.3 miles north of Canyon Junction (a 2.5 mile hike one-way).

DAY HIKES in the MADISON AREA

Harlequin Lake (easy/1.0 mile/30 minutes)
This easy stroll gives the hiker up-close exposure to lodgepole pines and a small marshy area commonly inhabited by waterfowl. The trailhead is located 1.5 miles west of the Madison Campground along the road from the West Park Entrance.

Two Ribbons Trail (easy/1.5 mile/30 minutes)
The park service has provided a boardwalk for the entire 1.5 mile. The trail basically follows along the Madison River and provides a look at burned lodgepole pine as well as Mother Nature's recovery and regrowth after a massive fire. The trailhead is located five miles east of the West Entrance to Yellowstone. You must look for the beginning

of the boardwalk in the large pullout; there is no official marking of the trailhead.

Purple Mountain (moderate/6.0 miles/3–4 hours)

This is another option for up-close exposure to burned lodgepole pine forests. The trail requires a climb of fifteen hundred feet and also provides views of the Firehole Valley. The trailhead can be found .25 mile north of Madison Junction on the Madison–Norris Road.

DAY HIKES in the MAMMOTH AREA

Lava Creek (moderately strenuous/3.5 miles/3–4 hours)

This trail follows Lava Creek past Undine Falls and eventually crosses the Gardner River before a rather steep climb near the end. The trail terminates near the Mammoth Campground. The trailhead is located across the road from the Lava Creek picnic area on the Mammoth–Tower Road.

Bunsen Peak (moderately strenuous/4.2 miles/2–3 hours)

This is yet another chance to hike through both meadow and forestland and terminates at the top of Bunsen Peak. Here you will get your well-earned views of Blacktail Plateau, the Gallatin Mountains, and the Yellowstone River Valley. The trailhead is located five miles south of Mammoth on the Mammoth–Norris Road directly across from the Glen Creek trailhead.

Beaver Ponds Loop (moderately strenuous/ 5.0 miles/2–3 hours)

Here is yet another opportunity to find meadow and forests. However, this trail offers excellent opportunities to view various animals as well. The trail starts north of Mammoth Terraces with a 350-foot ascent up above Clematis Gulch. Then, at the junction with Sepulcher Mountain Trail, you will head to the right. Shortly after this point, look for beaver, elk, mule deer, various birds, black bear, and grizzly bear. The tail then travels through forest and eventually back to Mammoth. The trailhead is located between Liberty Cap and the stone house next to Mammoth Terraces.

Again, think prior to your trip about how you plan to react if you see bear. If you are not prepared, do not hike at Yellowstone. Continually make noise, travel with others, carry bear spray, quickly stand close together with your fellow hikers if you encounter bear, ask park rangers for guidance and ask them specifically if they suggest any differences in how you should respond if you are attacked by black bear versus a grizzly bear. Again, park rangers are your best source of guidance in this area. This is not meant to scare anyone. The bears are not to be desperately feared, but definitely to be respected and to be provided their space. If you know what to do, AND WHAT NOT TO DO, you should be fine and have a fantastic time hiking. I have hiked most every western national park, including those in grizzly country such as Yellowstone and Glacier National Parks. I have encountered bear many times; however, due to my knowing what to do and how to react, I have never had a close encounter or been in a situation where I felt threatened. More on this in chapter eleven.

Osprey Falls Trail Sign

Osprey Falls (strenuous/8.0 miles/5–6 hours)

Admittedly, your author has not traveled all of the trails described in this book. However, of the ones I have done, this is probably my favorite. This hike can be divided into two parts. First, a flat section gets you to the top of the Osprey Falls Trail, and then the second section, a dramatically different terrain involving a steep descent and then a short hike around a rock corner for excellent and up-close views of the falls. The trail begins on an old dirt road worn down on just two tire lanes that travel along for 2.5 miles. At this point, there is a sign marking a turn to the right for Osprey Falls. Here the trail changes and descends seven hundred feet into a deep canyon named Sheepeater Canyon. After rounding a couple of rock outcroppings, you will get an excellent view of Osprey Falls falling 150 feet to the Gardner River below. This is an excellent spot for a backpack lunch! There is a lot of solitude on this trail. This is both good and bad, considering you are in bear country! The trailhead can be found south of Mammoth on the Mammoth–Norris Road directly across from the Glen Creek trailhead.

Osprey Falls

Rescue Creek (moderately strenuous/8.0 miles/5–6 hours)

You must first follow the Blacktail Deer Creek Trail past Blacktail Pond and then up a hill before turning left onto Rescue Creek Trail. Here you'll find a moderate climb through meadow and Aspen forests before descending to sagebrush and on to cross the Gardner River. Find this trailhead located seven miles east of Mammoth on the Mammoth-Tower Road.

Sepulcher Mountain (strenuous/11.0 miles/6–8 hours)

This hike first follows the Beaver Ponds Loop Trail to arrive at the start of the Sepulcher Mountain Trail. The trail then climbs sharply over 3,400 feet through (you guessed it) meadows and forest to the top of Sepulcher Mountain at 9,652 feet. The trail then loops around the back side of the mountain until it connects with the Snow Pass Trail, then descends to the Howard Eaton Trail, and then on to Mammoth Terraces and back to where you began the hike. The trailhead is located between Liberty Cap and the stone house next to the Mammoth Terraces.

Blacktail Deer Creek/Yellowstone River (moderately strenuous/12.0 miles/6–8 hours)

This unique hike actually originates within the park boundary, yet ends outside of Yellowstone National Park in Gardiner, Montana. The trail shadows Blacktail Deer Creek and descends eleven hundred feet through Douglas fir forest until is arrives at the Yellowstone River. Continuing along you will cross the river on a suspension bridge before connecting with the Yellowstone River Trail. The trail continues along, passing Knowles Falls and eventually ending in Gardiner, Montana. The trailhead is located seven miles east of Mammoth along the Mammoth–Tower Road.

DAY HIKES in the NORRIS AREA

Monument Geyser Basin (easy – strenuous/2.0 miles/1.5 hours)

This hike begins with an easy walk along the Gibbon River, then abruptly changes and climbs sharply to its termination. This is an interesting mostly dormant thermal area. Not much active excitement here, yet some interesting dormant cones to observe. As with all thermal areas, be sure to stay on the trail. The trailhead is located five miles south of Norris Junction on the Norris-Madison Road, just south of the Gibbon River Bridge.

Grizzly Lake (moderate/4.0 miles/2 hours)

This trail passes through lodgepole pines burned in the fires of both 1976 and 1988. You will also pass through meadows en route to Grizzly Lake, which is surrounded by thick forests. The trailhead can be found one mile south of Beaver Lake on the Mammoth–Norris Road.

Artist Paint Pots (easy/1.0 mile/30 minutes)

This hike has the obligatory meadows and burned lodgepole pine forest. However, it also offers some of the more colorful hot springs and small geysers found anywhere within Yellowstone. You'll also find two mud pots at the top of the hill with closer access than you'll find at Fountain Paint Pots of the Lower Geyser Basin located between Old Faithful and Madison Junction. Again, as with all thermal areas, be sure not to stray off the trail. The trailhead is located 4.5 miles south of Norris on the Norris-Madison Road.

Wolf Lake Cutoff (moderate/6.0 miles/4-4.5 hours)

This hike provides access to Wolf Lake. The route passes Little Gibbon Falls and follows along the Gibbon River. This is not the most well-maintained trail in the park and has no official trailhead marker. Look for orange markers in the large pullout .25 miles east of the Ice Lake Trailhead on the Canyon–Norris Road.

Cygnet Lakes (easy/8.0 miles/3–4 hours)

This is another poor- to not-at-all-maintained trail. This hike takes the hiker to Cygnet Lakes and the meadows that surround the area, another trail through burned Lodgepole Pine forests. The trailhead is located in a pullout on the south side of the Norris–Canyon Road 5.5 miles west of Canyon Junction.

Solfatara Creek (Easy-moderate/13.0 miles/5–6 hours)

This hike is relatively flat and, therefore, easy hiking. However, is may be best described as a moderate hike due to its distance—13 miles roundtrip. This is a poorly marked, poorly worn trail through known bear country. Again, do not hike through bear country alone or without knowing how to "hike smart" in possible bear habitat or without bear spray. This is a good hike if you want to get away from other hikers. You'll follow Solfatara Creek to a junction with the Ice Lake Trail, then on to Whiterock Springs. The trail gets more difficult to follow from this point, as is follows a slight incline up to Lake of the Woods, passing Amphitheater Springs and Lemonade Creek. You'll find secluded thermal areas and the ever-present Lodgepole pine forests. The trail then ends at the road. There are two trailhead options, one at each end. Find them located at "Loop C" in the Norris Campground and .75 mile south of Beaver Lake Picnic Area along the Mammoth-Norris Road.

DAY HIKES in the OLD FAITHFUL AREA

Observation Point (strenuous/1.0 or 1.4 miles/1 hour)
It is hard for me to list a one-mile trail as strenuous, but this short hike does indeed head fairly steeply uphill. This hike is a must at Yellowstone, and you'll find that everyone else partakes in this hike as well. The trail begins just across the Firehole River just to the northeast of Old Faithful Geyser and climbs uphill for a great overlook down on the Old Faithful Geyser, the Old Faithful Inn, and the Upper Geyser Basin. The hike is 1.0 miles unless you take the route that juts off from Observation Point to go to Solitary Geyser. This option, returning via the Geyser Hill boardwalk totals 1.4 miles.

Mystic Falls (moderately strenuous/2.5 miles/3 hours)
This hike follows a creek and leads to seventy-foot-high Mystic Falls of the Little Firehole River. From this point, you can climb up switchbacks to an overlook of the Upper Geyser Basin. This trail also goes through bear management areas and therefore is normally closed until the last Saturday in May. The trailhead is located at the back of the Biscuit Basin boardwalk, two miles north of Old Faithful Junction.

Divide (moderately strenuous/3.4 miles/4 hours)
Here is a relatively nondescript trail through forestland up to the Continental Divide with views of Shoshone Lake. The trailhead can be found 6.8 miles south of Old Faithful Junction in a pullout on the right side of the road.

Queen's Laundry (moderate/4.1 miles/2 hours)

This trail follows the Sentinel Meadows Trail along the Firehole River before heading out into an open meadow area. Here you will see the remains of an old bathhouse at a place called "Queen's Laundry." Construction was begun in 1881 but was never completed on what would have been the first government building constructed for public use in a national park. Today this site is designated a National Historic Site. The trailhead is located at the end of Fountain Flat Drive, which is on the left side ten miles north of Old Faithful on the Old Faithful–Madison Junction Road. You must cross a footbridge over the Firehole River to find the trailhead.

Lone Star Geyser (easy/4.8 miles/2 hours)

This trail is shared by hikers and bicyclists alike and is built upon an old service road beside the Firehole River leading to Lone Star Geyser. Lone Star Geyser rises about forty-five feet into the air about once every three hours. The trailhead can be found 3.5 miles south of the Old Faithful Junction, just beyond the parking area for Kepler Cascades. An alternative route to Lone Star Geyser is another section of the now familiar Howard Eaton Trail. This route is considered to be moderately strenuous and travels about 5.8 miles round-trip. You will pass through both burned and unburned forest. To locate this trailhead, park at the Old Faithful Ranger Station, take the paved path across the Grand Loop Road, then take a couple of lefts and follow orange markers leading you to the trailhead.

Imperial Geyser/Fairy Falls (easy/6.3 miles/2.5–3.5 hours)

This hike takes you through forest to Fairy Falls, then on another .65 miles to Imperial Geyser, which has frequent, but not all that impressive eruptions. The trailhead is located in a parking area one mile south of the Midway Geyser Basin where you must cross a steel bridge and walk one mile to the trailhead. As with the Mystic Falls Trail, this area is also a bear management area and is therefore normally closed until the last Saturday in May.

Mallard Lake (moderately strenuous/6.8 miles/4–5 hours)
You first head east from the Old Faithful Lodge (not the Old Faithful Inn) across the Firehole River. You will pass hot springs and acres of partially burned lodgepole pine en route to Mallard Lake. The trailhead is located just across the Firehole River to the east side of the Old Faithful Lodge and Cabins (not the Old Faithful Inn).

Mallard Creek (strenuous/9.2 miles/5–7.5 hours)
This is an up-and-down trail full of anything but flat land through burned forest to Mallard Lake. The trailhead can be found in a pullout on the east side of the road, 3.8 miles north of Old Faithful Junction on the Old Faithful–Madison Road.

DAY HIKES in the TOWER AREA

Slough Creek (moderately strenuous/2.0 miles/1–3 hours)
This trail was once an old wagon trail and actually takes the hiker from Wyoming into Montana and eventually beyond the northern boundary of Yellowstone National Park into the Absaroka-Beartooth Wilderness. The trail begins with a strenuous ascent then gets much easier

as it continues through two large meadows along the way. Keep your eyes peeled for moose and bear. The trailhead is located along the dirt road to the Slough Creek Campground that juts off to the north off the Northeast Entrance Road east of Tower Junction. Parking is allowed next to the vault toilet where the road bears left.

Mount Washburn (strenuous/3.1 or 2.5 miles/3–6 hours)

Here is another hiking destination with two trail options. You can climb Mount Washburn from two directions, both with excellent long distant views. This is a good place to see bighorn sheep; however, storms are likely in this higher altitude. Bring rain gear and avoid high open areas when lightning is forecast or seen in the area. Trailheads are located at the Chrittenden Road Parking Area, 8.7 miles south of Tower Junction on the Tower Junction–Canyon Junction Road for a 2.5 mile one-way hike, and in the Dunraven Pass Parking Area, 13.6 miles south of Tower Junction on the Tower Junction–Canyon Junction Road for a 3.1 mile one-way hike.

Yellowstone River Picnic Area (moderate/3.7 miles/2–3 hours)

This hike takes you along the rim of the canyon of the Yellowstone River. This is a good place to see bighorn sheep, peregrine falcons, and osprey. There are nice views of overhanging cliffs and basalt columns. The trailhead is located at the Yellowstone River Picnic Area 1.25 miles northeast of Tower Junction along the Northeast Entrance Road.

Hellroaring (strenuous/4.0 miles/2–3 hours)

This trail begins sharply downhill to the Yellowstone River Suspension Bridge, then crosses a plateau and arrives at Hellroaring Creek. The day hike stops here but the trail continues for the long-distance overnight backpackers. The trailhead can be found 3.5 miles west of Tower Junction on the Tower Junction–Mammoth Road.

Lost Lake (moderate/4.0 miles/2–3 hours)

This is a loop trail that begins and ends behind the Roosevelt Lodge. The trail heads west past Lost Lake, curves north toward Mammoth Hot Springs and the Petrified Tree parking lot, and then continues to loop clockwise to return to Roosevelt Lodge. Along the way, enjoy views of Lost Lake, sagebrush, and wildflowers, plus the occasional beaver and black bear. Again, stay back one hundred yards from bear! The trailhead is located directly behind Roosevelt Lodge.

Garnet Hill (moderate/7.5 miles/4–5 hours)

This trail follows an old stagecoach road for a mile and a half to a cookout site. The path then continues along Elk Creek until it comes very close to the Yellowstone River. Here you'll find a fork in the trail. Take the right (east) fork on around Garnet Hill and back south where it follows an old horse trail and ends along the Northeast Entrance Road. From this point, hikers must walk along the edge of the road about .25 mile back to where the hike began. The trailhead is located about fifty yards north of Tower Junction along the Northeast Entrance Road. Parking is permitted in a parking lot east of the Tower Junction service station.

DAY HIKES in the GRANT VILLAGE and WEST THUMB AREAS

West Thumb Geyser Basin (easy/3/8 mile/30 minutes)

This short walk is entirely on a well-constructed boardwalk. The path provides up-close views of active geysers, dormant geysers, and hot springs situated at or very near the shore of Yellowstone Lake. This hike is wheelchair accessible. The trailhead is located at the West Thumb Geyser Basin parking lot .25 mile north of West Thumb Junction.

Duck Lake (moderate/1.0 mile/30 minutes)

This hike takes you up a hill for a view of both Duck and Yellowstone Lakes and exposure to the remains of the historic fires of 1988 that burned heavily in this part of the park. The trail continues to Duck Lake, the source of drinking water for the West Thumb area. The trailhead can be found at the end of the West Thumb Geyser Basin parking lot.

Yellowstone Lake Overlook (moderately strenuous/ 2.0 miles/1 hour)

This is a loop trail, taking hikers to an elevated meadow for views of the West Thumb of Yellowstone Lake and the Absaroka Mountains in the distance. The trail then begins to descend and travels through meadows, thermal features, and forest. The trailhead is located on your immediate right as you drive into the West Thumb Geyser Basin parking lot.

Riddle Lake (easy/4.8 miles/2–3 hours)

This trail offers yet another chance to hike through forest and meadows, but also a good spot to view elk and bear. The trail terminates at a beautiful, yet small lake named

Riddle Lake. This trail is in a bear management area and is closed until mid-July. It is highly recommended that you hike in groups of four or more, but it is not required; be careful! Again, know how to react if you encounter bear, carry bear spray, continuously make noise while hiking, and check before you begin this hike with a park ranger for updates on bear activity in the area. The trailhead is located approximately three miles south of the Grant Village intersection, south of the Continental Divide road sign.

Shoshone Lake (easy/6.0 miles/2–3 hours)
An easy hike but a fairly long-distance hike, the trail takes you through meadows to arrive at Yellowstone's second largest lake, and the largest backcountry lake in the park, Shoshone Lake. There is a good chance in this area to see sandhill cranes and moose. Be sure to turn around at this point if you are day-hiking. The trail continues on deep into Yellowstone's vast backcountry. The trailhead is located 8.8 miles west of the West Thumb Junction on the West Thumb–Old Faithful Road.

Lewis River Channel/Dogshead Loop (moderately strenuous/11.0 miles/6–8 hours)
This is another trail taking the hiker into Yellowstone's backcountry. Hike along the Lewis River Channel where you will hopefully see ospreys and eagles. The trail loops past Shoshone Lake and takes you back to where you began via the Dogshead Trail. Be careful not to lose track of how far you have hiked, as this trail provides the opportunity to continue on into the vast backcountry for the die-hard multi-day overnight hiker. Look for the trailhead five miles south of the Grant Village intersection, just north of Lewis Lake on the west side of the South Entrance Road.

Chapter 6

I DON'T WANT OR LIKE TO HIKE; WHAT ELSE CAN I DO?

Yellowstone offers more recreation options than I could possibly list. However, options include viewing the natural thermal features (geysers, pools, mud pots, steam vents, and hot springs), visiting waterfalls, the Grand Canyon of Yellowstone, and Fort Yellowstone, picnicking, fishing, horseback riding, attending ranger programs, ice skating, snowshoeing, cross-country skiing, backcountry skiing, snowmobiling, bike riding, bird watching, swimming, photography, and much more. Shopping is even an option, consisting of mostly souvenir items, from T-shirts to mugs and even fine art.

Mammoth Area Attractions

The main attraction here is the Mammoth Hot Springs. They are an unbelievable sight of water, steam, and color that can be seen far in the distance as you approach. They are formed by hot water that rises through limestone. As rock is dissolved by hot water, a chalky mineral substance surfaces and coats the terraces, giving this site its unique look (admittedly a very basic explanation; ask a park ranger for a more scientific one). While the water temperature is above the boiling point well below the surface, the water that reaches the surface is piping hot, yet has cooled to a much lower temperature well under two hundred degrees. While this thermal feature is well outside the caldera that is beneath Yellowstone and the source of the geysers and other thermal features, there exists a fault that delivers the steaming water from the same source to surface as the Mammoth Hot Springs.

The 45th Parallel crosses through Yellowstone National Park in the Mammoth area. There is a sign marking the location on the main road just north of the Gardner River; very close to the Wyoming/Montana border. The 45th Parallel marks the equidistant point halfway between the equator and the North Pole. The Continental Divide also crosses through Yellowstone.

Boiling River refers to a popular place where bathers enter the Gardner River where a hot spring, called Boiling River enters and warms the water. The site is easily found by looking for a parking area just south of the 45th Parallel sign on the east side of the road. A footpath leads you about a half mile from the parking lot to access this section of the river. Proper bathing attire is required and be prepared for closure of this area in late spring and early summer due to high water.

Fort Yellowstone is not the square wooded old west fort the name might suggest, but a community of military buildings and houses erected to provide proper shelter for the U.S. Calvary from the very harsh winters in this area. The site of these fine matching structures, obviously built with military precision, hit me by surprise the first time I visited the north section of the park. It looks nothing like the other sections of the park, especially differing from the Old Faithful area buildings in the southern part of Yellowstone. Since the cavalry left Yellowstone in 1918, Fort Yellowstone has served as the park's headquarters. Unfortunately, many visitors simply visit the southern sections of the park due to the worldwide fame of the geysers located in this area. Again, this massive park deserves the planning and time commitment needed to see it in its entirety. Do not skip the northern part of the park; you will surely realize in later years that you came this far, yet made the mistake of not seeing all Yellowstone has to offer.

You should also take a moment to drive to the northern most part of the park, actually into Montana, to the north entrance. Here, the entrance is marked by the very famous Roosevelt Arch. President Theodore Roosevelt happened to be visiting the park during construction of the arch and was asked to do the honors of laying the cornerstone; as a result, it was named after the president.

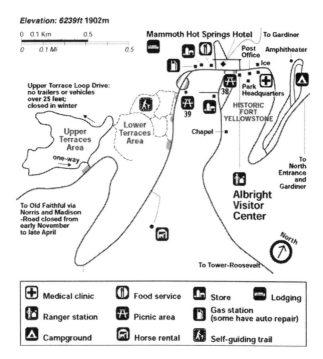

Mammoth Hot Springs Area

Madison Area Attractions

Madison's highlights are mainly thermal features and waterfalls. This is not known as a geyser area, but rather known for its springs and mud pots. The main thermal area here, Artist Paint Pots, is located just south of Norris Junction. A one-mile trail leads to numerous hot springs and large mud pots. You will also see heavily burned forest from the famous fires of 1988. In this area, you will also find Sylvan Springs, the Geyser Creek thermal area, and the Gibbon Hill Geyser Basin. The only well-known geyser area in this section of the park is a basically dormant basin called Monument Geyser Basin. You must walk a rather steep one-mile trail to see this area and its ghostly remains of a much more active period.

A must-see in this area is Gibbon Falls. This eighty-four-foot waterfall actually falls over the Yellowstone Caldera Rim.

Other sites worth seeing in the Madison area include Terrace Springs, a hot spring area located north of Madison Junction and accessible via boardwalks, forty-foot Firehole Falls and its swimming area, and the Madison Information Station. Information always makes for a safer and more efficiently planned vacation; however, the building itself is the main attraction here and is designated a National Historic Landmark.

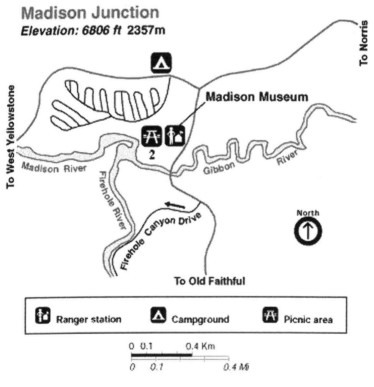

Madison Junction Area

Tower/Roosevelt Area Attractions

The main attraction in the area, in your author's opinion, would be the petrified trees. The Specimen Ridge located along the road, near the northeast entrance east of Tower Junction, is believed to be the largest concentration of petrified trees in the world. While much of this forest is hard to get up close to or get a good look at, the park has made it possible for you to get close to an excellent specimen. Near the Lost Lake Trailhead, "The Petrified Tree" is easily accessible via a basic road that begins about a mile from Roosevelt Lodge. Here you drive about a mile and a half to a parking area where you will see a petrified tree enclosed in a fenced area. The small fenced-in area may remind you of a small cemetery in old London out of some black and white Sherlock Holmes movie. There were once several specimens in this area, but the fence became necessary when visitors took so many illegal souvenirs that only the one specimen you see today was left standing.

Calcite Springs are steep cliffs of basalt located on the outside of a curve of the Yellowstone River downstream from The Grand Canyon of Yellowstone. These very steep chalky white cliffs are evidence of a lava flows from centuries back. This is an excellent spot in the park to view certain wildlife including bighorn sheep, bald eagles, plus various species of hawks and fish.

Tower Fall is a beautiful 132-foot fall along Tower Creek. The pinnacles surrounding the fall remind one more of the landscape common to other parks like Yosemite. National Park Service sites state that paintings of this natural feature by Thomas Moran helped inspire the federal government to establish the Yellowstone area as the first national park in 1872.

Hand-built sites to see include the Buffalo Ranch. The Lamar Buffalo Ranch was a necessary project constructed early in the twentieth century to assist in growing the buffalo (bison) population in an all-out effort to prevent extinction. This facility was operated through the 1950s and is today listed on the National Register of Historic Places. Four buildings remain today—two houses, a barn, and a bunkhouse.

The Northeast Entrance Ranger Station is also a National Historic Landmark. It, like the Old Faithful Inn, is considered an excellent example of what is called "parkitecture"; a common type of architecture used throughout the western national parks of the United States during the early parts of the twentieth century.

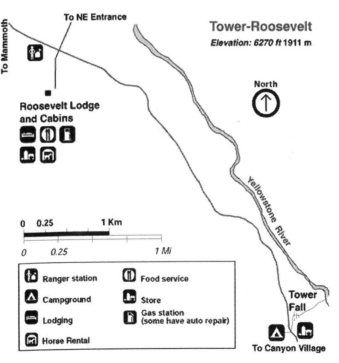

Tower Junction/Roosevelt Area

Norris Area Attractions

The Norris area contains the hottest and most hostile of all of Yellowstone's thermal sections. The Norris Geyser Basin is the site of the hottest temperature ever officially recorded at Yellowstone in a specially drilled hole at 459 degrees. This was not a surface temperature, but rather one recorded at 1,087 feet below the surface. The temperatures of most of the Norris area features are well above the boiling point, as water boils at about 199 degrees at this elevation. The most famous features in this area are Steamboat Geyser (the world's tallest at over 300 feet) and Echinus Geyser. STAY ON THE BOARDWALKS and well-marked associated dirt trails in this or any geyser area of Yellowstone. Thermal areas are very dangerous and foolish behavior can lead to severe scalding or death by falling into, drowning, and sinking hundreds of feet down into boiling thermal crevices. They are very beautiful, but remember the extreme conditions, namely the unbelievably hot water that creates their existence.

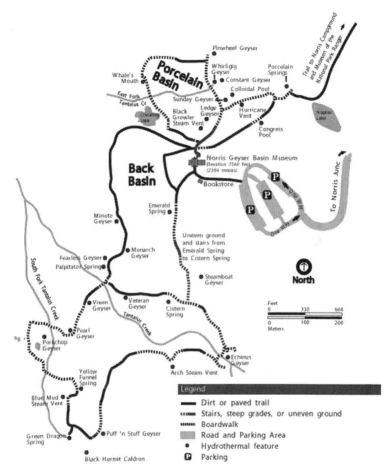

Norris Geyser Basin

Speaking of the boardwalks, there are many in this area that allow one to safely enjoy viewing the attractions. A three quarter mile dirt and boardwalk trail leads through the Porcelain Basin of trees, sound, color, and smell. A one and one-half mile trail of dirt and boardwalk leads visitors through the very heavily wooded Back Basin. There is a very acidic and dangerous section called the One Hundred Springs Plain where discovery and visitation is highly discouraged by the park service without their guidance and assistance.

Roaring Mountain is located just north of the Norris section and is a very large thermal area containing numerous steam vents called fumaroles. Located down an old road three miles off the main road is a viewpoint for a sixty-foot cascading waterfall named the Virginia Cascades of the Gibbon River.

The Norris area is located at the intersection of three fault lines. The Norris–Mammoth fault runs from Norris through Mammoth to Gardiner, Montana. The Hebgen Lake Fault runs from West Yellowstone, Montana, to Norris. The third fault is what is called a ring fracture caused by the Yellowstone Caldera about six hundred thousand years ago. The faults give the Norris area thermal features their unpredictability and extreme heat.

Finally, hand-built sites to see include the Norris Soldier Station and the Norris Geyser Basin Museum. The Norris Soldier Station serves as the Museum of the National Park Ranger and has been built, rebuilt, then built once again after fire, and modified or restored many times to get it to its present state. The Norris Geyser Basin Museum is a very attractive structure, made of stone and logs, and has been a park museum since it was completed in 1930.

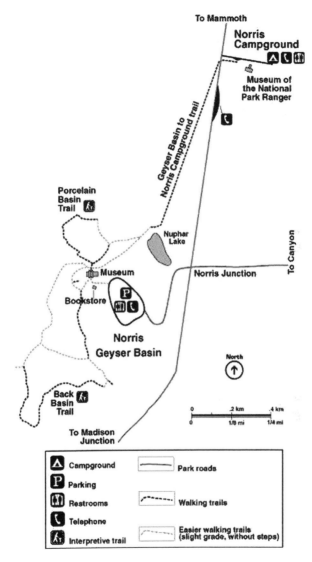

Norris Junction Area

**Lower Falls of the Grand Canyon of the
Yellowstone River**

Canyon Area Attractions

The main attraction in the Canyon area (as well as the entire park's most famous natural feature with the exception of Old Faithful Geyser) is the Grand Canyon of the Yellowstone River. At approximately twenty miles long, up to twelve hundred feet deep and four thousand feet wide, and over ten thousand years old, the erosion-created canyon is a sight you do not expect when traveling through Yellowstone. This is a prime example of the diversity and variety of sites to see in this unbelievable park: geysers, Mammoth Hot Springs, herds of bison, the Grand Canyon of the Yellowstone. What diverse variety!

The Canyon proudly displays two beautiful waterfalls; the Upper and Lower Falls of the Yellowstone River. The Upper Falls is 109 feet high and can be easily viewed from the Brink of the Upper Falls or from Uncle Tom's Trail. The Lower Falls is 308 feet high and can be easily viewed from various points including Artist Point, Red Rock Point, Lookout Point, and the Brink of the Lower Falls Trail. The Lower Falls is more than twice as high as Niagara Falls. The water volume flowing down the Yellowstone River and over the falls varies greatly by season from a peak of an estimated 63,500 gallons/second at peak spring runoff to a low of about 5,000 gallons/second in mid fall. The Yellowstone River eventually dumps into the Missouri River and is the longest undammed river in the continental United States.

Hayden Valley

The Hayden Valley of the Canyon Area is one of the very best places in Yellowstone to view wildlife. Spring brings large herds of bison that remain in this valley for much of the year, specifically spring, summer, and fall. Coyote is very common in this area as well. Grizzly bear can sometimes be seen in this area preying on the newborn elk and bison.

Also in this area is Mount Washburn, rising 10,243 feet. This is a good location for spotting bighorn sheep and was named after General Henry Dana Washburn who led the Washburn/Langford/Doane Expedition through this area in 1870.

The park visitor centers are full of great displays and movies explaining the science behind the thermal activity, the erosion along the Yellowstone River, the caldera, volcanic mountains, and more. I am certainly not a scientist and will not bore you with my limited understanding. However, the colors, and especially the brilliant golden color that is so often present and especially visible in the canyon area, is the result of iron, not sulfur. The National Park Service states that the canyon is basically "rusting."

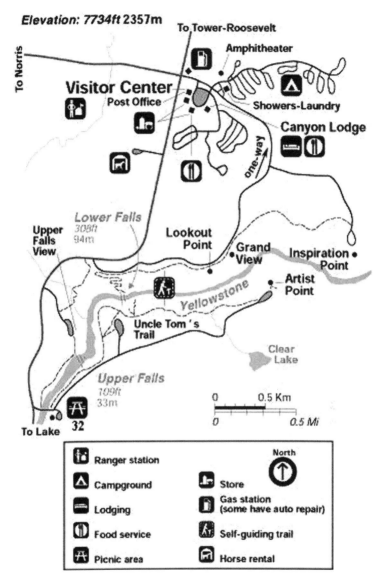

Elevation: 7734ft 2357m

To Tower-Roosevelt

Amphitheater

To Norris

Visitor Center

Post Office

Showers-Laundry

Canyon Lodge

one-way

Lower Falls
308ft
94m

Upper
Falls
View

**Lookout
Point**

Grand
View

Inspiration
Point

Artist
Point

Yellowstone

**Uncle Tom's
Trail**

Clear
Lake

Upper Falls
109ft
33m

To Lake 32

0   0.5 Km

0   0.5 Mi

North

Ranger station

Campground

Lodging

Food service

Picnic area

Store

Gas station
(some have auto repair)

Self-guiding trail

Horse rental

Canyon Junction Area

Yellowstone Lake

Lake Area Attractions

The major attractions in the Lake Area are Yellowstone Lake and the Yellowstone River. Yellowstone Lake is the highest high-altitude lake in North America; it is 7,733 feet above sea level. It has 110 miles of shoreline, about 141 square miles of surface area, and is roughly 20 miles north/south by 14 miles wide. However, this lake is mostly within the circular boundary of the park's caldera and therefore is filled with similar thermal features. The bottom of the lake (as well as marked attractions along the shoreline) is filled with geysers, hot springs and canyons. The lake freezes over completely in winter, has an average yearly temperature of forty-one degrees, and as this clearly indicates, is extremely cold. Survival time is estimated at less than half an hour in these conditions and as a result, SWIMMING IS STRONGLY DISCOURAGED IN YELLOWSTONE LAKE. As if all this was not interesting enough, Yellowstone

Lake is also home to the largest number of cutthroat trout in North America.

The Yellowstone River originates southeast of Yellowstone Lake; however, it picks up in size and width as it emerges from the north edge of the lake at Fishing Bridge. It leaves the park near Gardiner, Montana, eventually connects into the Missouri River, which joins the Mississippi River, and eventually flows into the Atlantic Ocean via the Gulf of Mexico.

Pelican Valley (along with the Hayden Valley previously mentioned in the Canyon Area) is another great place to safely view grizzly bear, black bear, bison, and elk.

Mud Volcano is another natural feature located approximately six miles north of Fishing Bridge on the road to Canyon Junction. Here you will find a handicapped-accessible parking lot and a short half-mile loop trail taking you to Dragon's Mouth and Black Dragon's Caldron. These mud volcanoes can be described as the earth releasing belches of steam and flying mud. There is another feature in this area that is not open for "anytime you like, take off and explore it on your own" visitation. It is a huge mud pot called the "Gumper" and is located off the safe and strongly advised boardwalk trail. If this interests you, the park asks you to check with a park ranger at Fishing Bridge for the schedule of ranger-led walks to this fascinating spot. This southern end of Hayden Valley, located between the Canyon Junction and Lake areas is the best place in all of Yellowstone to see mud pots; the largest group is located here at Mud Volcano. Smaller mud pot areas can be found at the West Thumb Geyser Basin, Fountain Paint Pot, and Artist Paint Pots.

Just north of Mud Volcano is one of the most acidic springs in all of Yellowstone, named the Sulphur Caldron. It can be safely viewed from its well-constructed viewing deck.

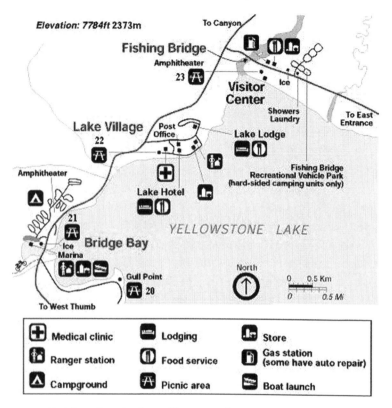

Bridge Bay/Lake Village/Fishing Bridge Areas

Grant Area Attractions

Other publications and Yellowstone personnel will tell you that Yellowstone Lake is shaped like a hand with several fingers and a thumb. Personally, I fail to see the resemblance. To me, it looks more like an octopus with a few legs missing. Whatever it reminds you of, the lower extensions are usually called arms with the western most called either the "West Thumb" or the "West Arm." This "West Thumb" is the site of another geyser basin, with its northern section referred to as the "Potts Basin." Here along the shoreline, and stretching from hundreds of yards away from the water to the same distance into the lake are springs and mini-geysers with a unique look, often tilting toward the water, projecting mud several feet into the air, or bubbling up from under water giving the lake water unique and widely varying colors from across the rainbow. Volcanic explosions thought to have occurred approximately 150,000 years ago formed this West Thumb. A much larger volcanic explosion occurred around 600,000 years ago forming the much larger main section of Yellowstone Lake. As these volcanic explosions occur, blowing off the cone, the aftermath is a collapsed or inverted cone, which then fills with water and forms lakes.

One standout hot spring in the West Thumb Geyser Basin is the "Abyss Pool." Then Chief Park Naturalist C.M. Bauer named it in 1935. He presumably got the name from the 1870 expedition notes of Lieutenant G.C. Doane who described his great visibility into this particular "deep abyss."

The Fishing Cone is another named and standout hot spring in the West Thump Geyser Basin. This feature gets its name from the Washburn Expedition of 1870. Cornelius Hedges, a member of the expedition, who had just caught a fish, in attempting to swing his trout ashore lost it off his hook and watched as it fell into the spring. When it surfaced, it was not only dead, but had been literally boiled. From this time on, it became a common visitor practice to replicate this act. From 1877 through 1882, Park Superintendent P.W. Norris demonstrated this feat for tourists often attracting large audiences. Today, park rules officially prohibit this practice, thought to be intrusive, unhealthy, and dangerous. You see, the cone is an active geyser and while it is infrequent, has been documented to erupt to heights of as much as forty feet and badly burned one person in 1921.

Lodgepole Pines are dominant throughout the Grant Area. The historic fires of 1988 were most prevalent in this area. There are numerous trails to take you through Lodgepole Forests including the Riddle Lake Trail, the Lake Overlook Trail, and the Duck Lake Trail. Here you will see the destruction Mother Nature is capable of up close; however, you will also see the natural reestablishment of the forests. Forest fires post a great threat to wildlife, hand-built (particularly historic) structures, and the natural beauty of the area; however, fire is natural, necessary, and in time shows how nature magically and all by itself, fully reestablishes its forests. More on this in chapter fifteen.

Little Thumb and Big Thumb creeks are spawning streams for cutthroat trout. Both grizzly and black bears migrate to this area during trout spawning season to feed.

The Continental Divide passes through this area at Craig Pass, approximately eight miles east of the Old Faithful area, nine miles west of the Grant Village/West Thumb area along the Grand Loop Road.

Other large lakes in this area include Shoshone Lake (the park's second largest after Yellowstone Lake), Lewis Lake, and Heart Lake. All of these lakes are under strict park regulations to both preserve their integrity and to prevent unwanted noise preserving the natural park experience. As a result, no motorized watercraft is permitted.

While the Snake River and the Snake River Canyon probably first bring neighboring Grand Teton National Park to mind as they comprise one of its most prominent features, the Snake River actually originates in Yellowstone National Park. Contrary to what many believe, the Snake River is not named as such because it "snakes" through the Grand Tetons, but rather the name comes from the Shoshone or Snake Indians and can be traced back as far as

1812. Forty-two miles of the river are within the boundaries of Yellowstone National Park.

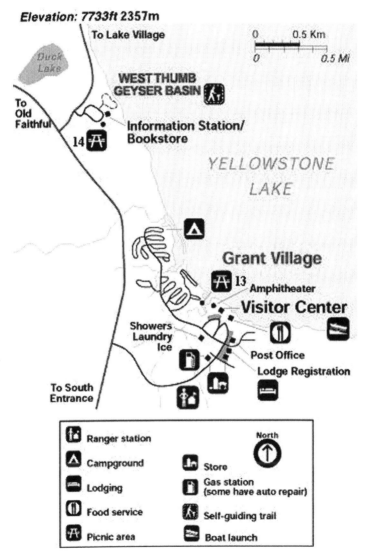

West Thumb and Grant Village Areas

Old Faithful Area Attractions

I saved the Old Faithful area for last for two reasons. First, it clearly has the most sites, both natural and hand built to see. Most of the geysers (the park's most famous and well-known features) are located in this area, as well as the most famous hand-built structure in the park—the Old Faithful Inn. Secondly, I want to give some strong advice here: DO NOT LIMIT YOUR YELLOWSTONE VACATION TO JUST THIS SECTION OF THE PARK! This is a common mistake. Many people have reached well into adulthood; have heard about the Old Faithful Geyser their whole life, and have "always wanted to see it." They finally get together the time, money, and travel plans to come to Yellowstone. They visit the Old Faithful Geyser, see the adjacent Old Faithful Inn, and return home telling everyone they've seen Yellowstone! As you have already learned, there is so much variety and so much more to see in this magnificent and gigantic park than just the Old Faithful area. Make no mistake, this is a real highlight, yet it represents just a small part of all this fantastic national park has to offer.

Old Faithful Geyser

Having gotten that off my chest, yes, the greatest concentration of geysers is in this area. Let's define "this area" as the immediate Old Faithful area plus points to the north along the Grand Loop road from Old Faithful at least halfway to Madison Junction. Old Faithful Geyser is very impressive. Park information states that she erupts up to 184 feet in the air with an average eruption of 130 feet. Eruptions usually last 1.5 to 5 minutes, with intervals of 65 minutes if the eruption lasts less the 2.5 minutes and intervals of 92 minutes if the eruption lasts more than 2.5 minutes. Water temperature is 203 degrees just prior to eruption (water boils at 199 degrees at this 7,366 feet of altitude) and she dispenses a water volume of 3,700 to 8,400 gallons with each eruption.

Most (but certainly not all) of the geysers in this area are divided into the Upper Geyser Basin and the Lower Geyser Basin. Upper and lower refer to the relative elevations of these sections, not north vs. south on the map. Therefore, the Upper Basin is actually just to the south of the Lower Basin. The Upper Basin begins practically just out the door of the Old Faithful Inn heading north, while the Lower Basin is just a few miles north along the Grand Loop Road going from the Old Faithful area toward Madison Junction. Yellowstone has close to sixty percent of the world's known geysers. The Upper Basin has the greatest number of geysers in the park and includes five of the six that the park actually posts predictions for the timing of eruptions. The Upper Basin is home to Castle, Daisy, Grand, Riverside, and Old Faithful geysers whose activity is predicted by park staff. The Lower Basin has the other predicted geyser, Great Fountain. Don't make the mistake of just focusing on these six geysers. Just because they are fairly predictable, does not necessarily mean they are the most magnificent or memorable. In fact, nearly everyone who visits Yellowstone can tell you about seeing Old Faithful go off. Wouldn't the bragging rights be better if you can tell your friends about seeing less-well-documented activity? This Upper Basin area is approximately one square mile and offers at least 150 individual thermal features. The Lower Basin is a much larger area with the thermal features somewhat more spread out. This area can be enjoyed on foot via a boardwalk trail whose trailhead begins at Fountain Paint Pots, or by car via a three-mile one-way drive named Firehole Lake Drive, which, as just mentioned, includes the sixth predicted geyser, Great Fountain Geyser. The Firehole Lake or Firehole Flats drive juts off the main Grand Loop Road just south of the Nez Perce picnic area.

Morning Glory Pool

As you walk the trails and boardwalks of the Upper Geyser Basin, you'll not only see magnificent geysers, but beautiful hot springs as well. One of the most beautiful is Morning Glory Pool. A 1959 earthquake caused its water to become somewhat cloudy for decades, but in recent years, it has returned to its trademark clarity and reflects the blue of the sky best when the sun is highest in the midday sky. Another great hot spring of the Upper Geyser Basin not to be missed is the Blue Star Spring.

Blue Star Spring

Other geyser basins in this section of the park include the Midway Geyser Basin, located, as the name implies, between the Upper and Lower geyser basins. The Midway Geyser Basin includes Yellowstone's largest hot springs, the Grand Prismatic Spring—approximately 370 feet in diameter and over 120 feet deep! Also located in this area is the Excelsior Geyser with a crater 200 by 300 feet and spouting over four thousand gallons of water per minute into the Firehole River.

The Lone Star Geyser Basin can be seen only by hiking a five-mile round trip whose trailhead is located just to the south of Old Faithful. It erupts approximately every three hours. The Shoshone Geyser Basin can be visited only by hiking a seventeen-mile round trip. This basin has no boardwalks and is considered dangerous. There are obvious worn trails that must be followed (DO NOT STRAY OFF THE MARKED TRAILS).

Other natural attractions in this area of the park include Craig Pass where the Continental Divide crosses through the park at 8,262 feet and Kepler Cascades. Kepler is a cascading waterfall cascading over 125 feet. There is a marked pullout just south of Old Faithful and it is easily accessible via a short walk.

The hand-built structures are another major attraction of the Old Faithful part of this park. Rarely in a national park is so much attention drawn to other than natural beauty. The basic premise of the national park system is preserving what Mother Nature made for future generations to enjoy. However, the historic buildings in this area are a major reason to be drawn to Yellowstone. The Old Faithful Inn is now over one hundred years old, having been built ironically during winter in 1903–1904. Designer Robert C. Reamer's huge structure is today a National Historic Landmark itself. While the National Park System is known for its beautiful and throwback great lodges, especially those of its western national parks, the two most famous are the Ahwahnee Hotel, located at Yosemite, and the Old Faithful Inn at Yellowstone. This rustic log structure is seven stories high, features a sixty-five-foot ceiling in its lobby, and one of the most beautiful and oversized stone fireplaces one will ever see. It is probably the best example of "parkitecture" anywhere and an absolute must-see!

Located near the Old Faithful Inn is the even older Lower Hamilton Store. It was originally built in 1897 as a photo studio and has been moved from its original site. Originally located just to the northwest of the front side of the Old Faithful Inn, today it stands near the intersection of Grand Loop Road and its fire lane.

The Old Faithful Lodge is not another name for the Old Faithful Inn, but rather another building that has evolved from its original structure. Having begun as a laundry faculty in 1918, today it is comprised of a cafeteria, coffee shop, gift shop, and check in desk for its cabin-style lodging.

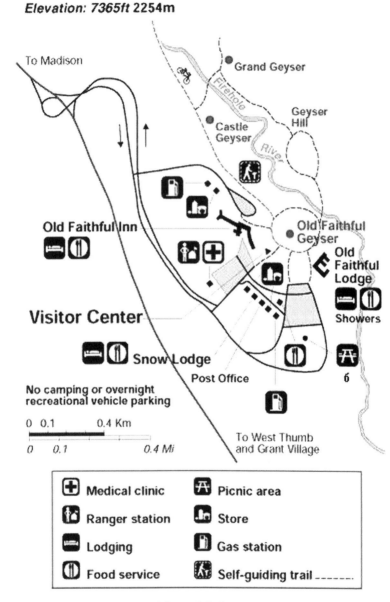

Elevation: 7365ft 2254m

To Madison

Grand Geyser

Firehole

Castle
Geyser

Geyser
Hill

River

Old Faithful Inn

Old Faithful
Geyser

Old
Faithful
Lodge

Visitor Center

Showers

Snow Lodge

Post Office

6

**No camping or overnight
recreational vehicle parking**

To West Thumb
and Grant Village

0   0.1   0.4 Km

0   0.1   0.4 Mi

Medical clinic — Picnic area

Ranger station — Store

Lodging — Gas station

Food service — Self-guiding trail ------

Old Faithful Area

Picnicking was made for this park. Picnicking is all about making your own meal and eating it in a beautiful outdoor setting with friends, family, and nature. This is certainly in keeping with the national park concept and Yellowstone certainly has infinite locations and settings for the perfect picnic. At last count, there were fifty official Yellowstone National Park picnic areas located throughout the park. There are multiple locations on every connecting arm of the Grand Loop and on each of the five entrance roads. Having said this, it would be impractical to list each location here. You can go to the park Web site at www.nps.gov/yell/planyourvisit/picnic.htm to get a complete listing that includes the number of tables at each site, whether a particular site has fire grates and restrooms, and whether or not the restrooms are handicap accessible. Madison is the only picnic site that provides water. A map of all fifty picnic sites can be found at www.nps.gov/yell/planyourvisit/upload/455Picnico8.pdf.

A few picnic rules that must be complied with for your safety, animal safety, and to prevent forest fires:

- Fires are allowed only if fire grates are provided.
- Liquid or gas self-contained charcoal grills may be used for food preparation.
- Feeding animals (including birds) is illegal.
- Food and drink cannot be left unattended at any time.
- Camping is not allowed in the picnic areas.

Bicycling in Yellowstone is a great way to get around and something the kids will especially enjoy. You can bring your own or rent bicycles from Xanterra Parks & Resorts at Old Faithful. While bicycling is fun, remember that elevations range from 5,300 to 8,860 feet and services and facilities are very far apart, often up to thirty miles. There are many routes restricted to bicycle and foot traffic only in the Mammoth, West Entrance, Old Faithful, Lake, and Tower areas. Get specifics at www.nps.gov/yell/planyourvisit/bicycling.htm.

～

Horseback riding and Llama Packing are available as well from Xanterra Parks & Resorts. Offered are horse rides of one and two hours in length available at Tower-Roosevelt and Canyon, with Mammoth offering only one-hour rides. The Mammoth Corral also offers the previously mentioned horseback or wagon rides that take visitors to the Old West Dinner Cookouts. They strongly encourage advance reservations for any of these activities, which can be made by calling 307-344-7311. Get more information including dates of operation and current pricing at www.nps.gov/yell/planyourvisit/horseride.htm.

～

Outboard boats and rowboats are available for rent on a first-come, first-served basis on Yellowstone Lake. Guided fishing boats can be reserved in advance through Xanterra by calling 307-344-7311. There are concessionaires offering canoeing, kayaking, and motorized boating.

Private boating is also allowed on Yellowstone Lake via launching ramps at the Bridge Bay Marina. A permit must be obtained for all motorized and non-motorized vessels, including float tubes. They must be obtained in person at one of four locations: the South Entrance, the Lake Lewis Campground, the Grant Village Backcountry Office, or the Bridge Bay Ranger Station. Permits for non-motorized boating can also be obtained at the West Entrance, Northeast Entrance, Canyon Backcountry Office, Old Faithful Backcountry Office, Mammoth Backcountry Office, Bechler Ranger Station, West Contact Station, or the West Yellowstone Chamber of Commerce. Cost is $20 for a yearly permit or $10 for a seven-day permit. Permits issued in Grand Teton National Park are also good in Yellowstone but the vessel must still be registered in Yellowstone; you will receive a free Yellowstone validation sticker. Pleasure crafts such as Jet Skis, airboats, and submersibles are not permitted in the park.

⁓

For evening entertainment, remember that you will not get much in the way of radio or television reception in the park. Actually, you can get television, but only in two suites at the Mammoth Hot Springs Hotel. I remember a radio in our room one visit at Grant Village; however, the only station we got was the park information station, which repeats every few minutes. Having said all this, do you really want to travel to a national park to watch television?

My family and I always take in as many evening ranger talks as possible. They are offered at various locations throughout the park. Locations, times, and topics change very regularly and with the seasons. Best to check the park newspaper *Yellowstone Today*, which you should receive from the gate ranger when you enter the park, ask at your lodging locations front desk, ask at any visitor center, or ask any park ranger. Locations for evening lectures/slide shows include the Norris Campground Campfire Circle, Madison Campground Amphitheater, Canyon Campground Amphitheater, Grant Visitor Center Auditorium, the benches in front of the Old Faithful Visitor Center, and in front of the Albright Visitor Center at Mammoth Hot Springs (inside theater if raining). Limited dates exist for programs at the West Yellowstone Visitor Information Center. You are welcome to attend any location or program regardless of where you are lodging; each site will have a different topic on any given night. These are free interactive lectures, talks, or slide shows, lasting about an hour. They are incredibly informative, relaxing, and the perfect way to wind down the day. Daily topics are often on a several day (i.e., seven-day) rotation and may include presentations on geothermal features, wildlife, fires in the park, changing seasons, the first park settlers, early mining in the park, etc.

~

A drive through Yellowstone can easily fill an entire day. By the way, be sure you have plenty of gas; Yellowstone is a big place with lots of isolated areas and very cold nights much of the year. You can tank up at any one of seven locations within the park. Gas is available at Canyon, Fishing Bridge, Grant Village, Mammoth, Tower Junction, Upper Old Faithful, and Lower Old Faithful. It would be impossible to list all the options for a day trip through the park. Suffice it to say a common mistake people make is driving in a short distance from one entrance and thinking they've seen Yellowstone. This park, as much as any, has many varied areas. There is nothing wrong with preferring certain parts of this park, or any park, but you are cheating yourself if you do not look around on your first trip to make sure you know all that is here. Certainly everyone will have his or her favorite part of this very large park; visitors, those who work in the park, those who love hiking, those who love the historic lodges most, etc. will all have differing preferences and all are absolutely justified. However, most would agree that the main sections of the park are the Old Faithful Inn, the fabulous geothermal sites featuring the geyser basins stretching from Old Faithful to Madison Junction to Norris Junction, Yellowstone Lake, the Grand Canyon of Yellowstone section of the Yellowstone River at Canyon Village, and the Mammoth Hot Springs area. Please do not be one who passes through the North Entrance and sees only the Mammoth Hot Springs, enters through the South Entrance and visits only the Old Faithful Inn and watches Old Faithful erupt one time, or enters through the West Entrance and visits only a couple of geyser basins near Madison Junction. Get in the car, start out early, and travel through the entire park. It may take a week to ten days to take a good bite out of all that exists here; however, a well-planned day will get you a decent stop at all these locations to at least have a taste, know what is here, make knowledgeable plans for the days you have, or know what you want to return to see more fully on another visit and at a more relaxing pace.

You can even get married at Yellowstone National Park. Weddings are permitted at various locations inside the park including the Old Faithful area, the Lake Butte Overlook, and the Grand Canyon of the Yellowstone River. A special park permit is required (unless the ceremony is held in the Mammoth Chapel) as well as abiding by the entrance fee policies. A permit application must be received in the park at least two weeks prior to the wedding date. Applications cost $50 and can be obtained from and returned to the Visitor Services Office along with the nonrefundable payment. The address is:

Visitor Services Office
P.O. Box 168
Yellowstone National Park, WY. 82190

Ceremonies in the Mammoth Chapel do not require the $50 application fee; however, they do require a $100 fee to reserve the chapel. Reservations must be made through the Superintendent's Office at 307-344-2003.

Either a Wyoming or a Montana marriage license is required, depending on the location(s) of the ceremony in the park. A Montana license is applicable if the ceremony will be held near Mammoth Hot Springs and a Wyoming license for most other locations that are more in the interior of the park. For a Montana license, call Livingston at 406-222-4125; the cost is $53. For a Wyoming license, call either Cody at 307-527-8600 or Jackson Hole at 307-733-7733; the cost is $25. The minimum age in both states is eighteen!

Chapter 7

VISITOR CENTERS, RANGER PROGRAMS, MEDICAL FACILITIES, SERVICE STATIONS, STORES, AND MORE

Yellowstone National Park Visitor Centers are located at Mammoth (Albright Visitor Center & Museum), Canyon (Canyon Visitor Education Center), Lake (Fishing Bridge Museum & Visitor Center), Grant Village (Grant Village Visitor Center), Madison (Madison Information Station), Norris (Norris Geyser Basin Museum), and Old Faithful (Old Faithful Visitor Education Center).

The **Albright Visitor Center at Mammoth** is located at Mammoth Hot Springs, five miles south of the park's North Entrance. The building used for the visitor center along with many others at Mammoth, was built by the United States Calvary and was originally part of "Fort Yellowstone." The visitor center includes a museum and a theater. The theater shows interesting and informative films every half hour in summer and by request in winter. Films are subject to change but have recently included "The Challenge of Yellowstone" (twenty-five minutes on the history of the park and the evolution of the national park concept), "Thomas (Yellowstone) Moran" (twelve minutes on Moran's contributions to the creation of Yellowstone as the first national park), and "Yellowstone Today" (eighteen minutes on all that Yellowstone offers visitors during the summer months.

The **Canyon Visitor Education Center** focuses on the supervolcano that is Yellowstone. Visitors can view interactive exhibits, data, and videos that explain and educate the park visitor on the Yellowstone volcano, geysers, hot springs, and other thermal features of this monstrous park. Currently showing is a new film on the geology of Yellowstone entitled "Land to Life," a room-size relief model of the park showing volcanic eruptions, lava flows, glaciers, and faults that are the reasons for Yellowstone's uniqueness, a nine-thousand-pound rotating ball illustrating the world's volcanic activity, and much more. The center even houses one of the world's largest lava lamps illustrating how magma rises to the earth's surface. This is a very new facility which first opened its doors in August 2006.

The **Fishing Bridge Museum &Visitor Center (Lake Area)** is located one mile east of the intersection of the Grand Loop with the East Entrance Road on the East Entrance Road. The building is designated a National Historic Landmark. Built in 1931 and designed of stone and log architecture or "parkitecture," the center features taxidermied animals including birds, grizzly bear, and river otters. There are no video or auditorium facilities at this location. There is a Yellowstone Association Bookstore located here.

The **Norris Geyser Basin Museum** serves as a visitor center for the Norris area. It is located .25 mile east of Norris Junction on the Norris Junction–Canyon Junction Road. It features an even earlier example of the stone and log architecture known as "parkitecture," built in 1929–1930 and is often credited as the original example and model for all future use of this type of park architecture built across the nation, particularly in the great western parks. This site houses exhibits on geothermal geology and specific features of the Norris Geyser Basin. There are no video or auditorium facilities at this location. There is a Yellowstone Association Bookstore located here.

The **Grant Village Visitor Center** can be found on the shore of the West Thumb of Yellowstone Lake, one mile east of the South Entrance Road just south of West Thumb. It is named for President Ulysses S. Grant who signed the bill making Yellowstone the country's and the world's first national park in 1872. The construction of this entire Grant Village area in the 1970s was very controversial due to its location in grizzly bear habitat. The bears roam this area because they depend upon the cutthroat trout spawning streams located in this area for their food. This visitor center primarily features exhibits meant to educate visitors on the role of fire in Yellowstone and other national parks. A movie called "Ten Years after Fire" is shown regularly during the summer. The Yellowstone Association has a book sales area at this site as well.

The **Madison Information Station** was built during 1929–1930 along with the previously discussed Norris Geyser Basin Museum and is a National Historic Landmark as well. It can be found in the Madison Junction Picnic Area. Legend states that it sits on the site of the legendary campfire circle built by the Washburn-Langford-Doane Expedition. After years of sitting empty, it reopened as an information center and Yellowstone Association bookstore in 1995. This is a more limited visitor center than the ones previously discussed.

The **Old Faithful Visitor Education Center** is a brand-new facility having replaced the previous Old Faithful Visitor Center with a high-tech twenty-seven million dollar facility which opened to the public in August 2010. The park claims the new facility is designed to set new standards for accessibility and for the presentation and interpretation of complex scientific information. This visitor center expects to see 2.6 million visitors walk through its doors annually. The building contains exhibits to help visitors better understand hydrothermal features including geysers and hot springs. On-site facilities include an auditorium, research library, multi-purpose classroom and bookstore. The Yellowstone Association has their largest and most complete selection of sales merchandise here at Old Faithful.

$\approx$

Backcountry Offices are park ranger-staffed facilities that issue backcountry camping, boating, and fishing permits, offer emergency services, as well as general park and updated wildlife information. Backcountry offices are located inside the visitor center at Mammoth, at ranger stations at Lake and Bay Bridge, across the parking lot from the visitor center at Old Faithful, and at the Tower Ranger Station. There is also an intermittently staffed location, in spring and fall before and after the visitor center is open for the season at Grant Village.

$\approx$

Ranger-led Programs are unbelievably numerous, very well done, and available at all the major areas of the park. For example, you can meet with a ranger at the Artist Point Overlook or walk along the South Rim Trail of the Grand Canyon of Yellowstone in the Canyon area. You can take a narrated lake cruise on Yellowstone Lake (charge for this activity available through Xanterra Parks and Resorts by stopping by the Bridge Bay Marina or calling 307-344-7311) or learn about odd creatures living at Yellowstone from a park ranger at the Fishing Bridge Visitor Center. You can walk the West Thumb Geyser Basin along the shores of Yellowstone Lake with a ranger. Available are ranger-led discussions of geology, history, and wildlife, or educational discussions of why elk congregate in the Mammoth area. There is a morning walk with a ranger on Geyser Hill or a half-day ranger-led hike into the backcountry ($15 adults and $5 for children ages seven–fifteen) originating in the Old Faithful area.

These are just a taste of the many programs available for your enjoyment while vacationing at Yellowstone. The program schedule is always subject to change and changes by season. The last time I checked, the fall season alone included twenty-seven different ranger-led programs. Obviously, the summer options are even more numerous. The best source for a complete listing of available programs is the official newspaper of Yellowstone National Park, *Yellowstone Today*.

Having said this, the programs I highly recommend, which my family and I take in every time we visit any national park, are the evening ranger presentations/discussions. These are usually offered at auditoriums in Visitor Centers, at outdoor amphitheaters at campgrounds, and sometimes at the larger lodges. They are free, usually last about an hour, and are most often slide shows or PowerPoint presentations with accompanying Q&A on topics ranging from early settlers, to wildlife, to fire in the park, to the four seasons in the park, and much more. They differ each evening with usually four to seven programs in the rotation. This is a very enjoyable way to wind down the day after dinner and before bed. You will not be receiving radio or television in the park. Your evening entertainment options are pretty much these excellent programs, or the deck of cards you brought from home.

~

Medical facilities are available at three locations: Lake/Bay Bridge, Old Faithful, and Mammoth Hot Springs. The Mammoth location is open year-round while the other two are seasonal facilities open from mid-May through late September (Lake/Bay Bridge) or early October (Old Faithful). Old Faithful does have some intermittent winter hours; you can call the Mammoth clinic to make an appointment. The phone numbers appear in chapter nine. These professionally staffed facilities offer emergency care and more. My wife once visited the clinic at Old Faithful and a similar facility at Grand Teton National Park on one of our summer vacations for a nonemergency medical need. She was treated very professionally, provided all the care she required with the necessary equipment and medicine on the premises. These facilities treat everything from emergencies arising from accidents while in the park, to common medical needs like the flu and allergies. They have X-ray, some lab, and pharmacies in-house. The Mammoth location is staffed by a board-certified physician. The other locations may be staffed by a physician or a nurse practitioner. They can provide first-response assistance for more serious medical needs and can arrange transportation to larger facilities in towns and cities outside the park.

∾

A few quick comments on **shopping**. You'd be surprised at all that is available for purchase in Yellowstone National Park. No, this is not Manhattan, or even Chicago's Michigan Avenue, but there is more available here than you would probably expect. There are General Stores, offering groceries, a restaurant, camping and fishing gear, and souvenirs at Canyon Village, Fishing Bridge, Grant Village, Lake, Tower, and two locations at Old Faithful (lower and upper locations). There is a General Store at Mammoth but this location does not have a restaurant within the store (there are restaurants at Mammoth though). There are Gift Shops in the Canyon Lodge, Grant Village Lodge, Lake Yellowstone Hotel, Lake Lodge, Mammoth Hot Springs Hotel, Old Faithful Inn, Old Faithful Snow Lodge, and the Roosevelt Lodge. There is a second general-type store referred to as a "mini-store" at Grant Village offering groceries, souvenirs, as well as a limited inventory of camping and fishing gear. Outdoor Stores, offering everything you may need in recreation gear (hiking, camping, fishing, winter sports, etc.) plus snacks, souvenirs, and fast food, are located at Bridge Bay and Canyon Village. Note that most of these sites are open from sometime in May through late September or early October.

∾

Service stations are available at seven locations throughout the park. Full service locations offering gas, diesel, repair, and wrecker services are located at Canyon

101

Village, Fishing Bridge, and Grant Village. The Upper Old Faithful site offers gas, repair, and wrecker services. Mammoth and Lower Old Faithful offer fuel (gas and diesel) only. Tower Junction offers gas only. Propane can be obtained at Fishing Bridge and Grant Village.

≈

United States post offices are located at Mammoth Hot Springs, Old Faithful, Grant Village, Canyon Village, and Lake. The Mammoth location is open year-round Monday through Friday, except holidays from 8:30 a.m. to 5:00 p.m. Seasonal months of operation for the other sites are: Old Faithful (early May through late October), Grant Village (mid-May through mid-September), Lake Village (mid-May through mid-October), and Canyon Village (late May through mid-September).

Chapter 8

TOURS, TRANSPORTATION, AND OTHER ACTIVITIES

Numerous tours are available. In fact, it is mind boggling just how many options and vendors are available to assist you in seeing all Yellowstone has to offer. I will list several Web sites so you can dig deeply into all the options, if you please. However, I will list some of the details for tours and activities available through Xanterra Parks & Resorts. Most tours require a minimum of three paying passengers for the tour to take place. All tours offer reduced rates for children eight–fifteen years of age while children seven and under are free. Listed are the 2010 adult price followed by the children's price in parenthesis. Also, prices do not include tax, utility fee, or gratuity.

Most all of the tours listed here require advance reservations, which can be made by calling 866-GEYSERLAND (866-439-7375) or 307-344-7311. Additional information can be found at either www.yellowstonenationalparklodges.com/summer-tours-activities-256.html or www.yellowstonenational parklodges.com/Interpretive-Tours-256_1362.html.

Xanterra offers both modern bus/van tours, as well as tours via Historic Yellow Buses. These beautiful buses have a lengthy history of use as far back as the 1930s in Yellowstone and other national parks, but in 2007 they were refurbished and updated to meet today's standards for safety and emissions. These are sister vehicles to the red versions you may be familiar with that are once again in use north of Yellowstone at Glacier National Park. If none of the following tours fit your needs, there is the option of a Custom Guided Tour, available via Interpretive Bus/ Van, Historic Old Yellow Bus, or winter Snowcoach. These typically last eight to twelve hours and comprise individual tours planned directly with the guest. Check the Web sites listed in the previous paragraph for a complete listing of Custom Guided Tour options and pricing. Pricing is usually set as a flat price for the first five hours plus a per hour additional charge for each additional hour.

Interpretive Bus/Van Tours offered within the park by Xanterra are the Yellowstone in a Day Tour, the Circle of Fire Tour, the Washburn Expedition Tour, and the Lamar Valley Wildlife Excursion Evening Tour. Three of these are all-day tours while the Lamar Valley Wildlife Excursion lasts four to just over six hours depending on departure location.

Historic Old Yellow Bus Tours offered within the park by Xanterra are quite varied and include all-day tours, partial-day tours, and evening tours. The all-day tours are the Teton Vista Rendezvous (Monday, Wednesday, Friday) and Yellowstone in a Day (Tuesday, Thursday). Partial Day Tours are Wake Up To Wildlife, Picture Perfect Photo Safari, Firehole Basin Adventure, and Geyser Gazers. Evening Tour offerings are the Lake Butte Sunset Tour, Evening Wildlife Encounters, and Twilight on the Firehole Tour.

The Yellowstone in a Day Tour (via Interpretive Bus/Van)

This all-day tour lasts up to eleven hours and offers just what the name implies—a great overview of the entire park. Included is most every park highlight including Old Faithful, Yellowstone Lake, the Grand Canyon of the Yellowstone River, and much more. Lunch is not included in the ticket price. This tour operates from late May through mid-September departing from Gardiner, Montana, and Mammoth. Tickets are $70 ($35) from Gardiner and $68 ($34) from Mammoth.

The Circle of Fire Tour (via Interpretive Bus/Van)

This all-day tour runs approximately nine hours. It travels the lower loop of Yellowstone's figure eight loop road system. You'll see the Upper and Lower Geyser Basins, the Norris Geyser Basin, Yellowstone Lake, and the Grand Canyon of the Yellowstone River. The tour stops at varying locations for lunch (lunch not included). The tour operates from late May through mid-September. Departure locations are Canyon Lodge, Lake Yellowstone Hotel, Old Faithful Inn, Grant Village, Fishing Bridge RV Park, and the Bridge Bay Campground. Tickets cost $63 ($31.50).

The Washburn Expedition Tour (via Interpretive Bus/Van)

This all-day tour lasts from just under six to just over eight hours depending on the location you depart from. This is a modern-day version of the trek General Henry Washburn's expedition traveled with stops at the Grand Canyon of the Yellowstone River and Denraven Pass. Plan on lots of wildlife, scenery, and geology. Departure locations are Bridge Bay Campground, Lake Yellowstone

Hotel, Fishing Bridge RV Park, and Canyon Lodge. This tour is offered late May through mid-September, beginning early June from Canyon Lodge (Canyon Village). The price is $57 ($28.50), $51 (25.50) from Canyon Lodge.

The Lamar Wildlife Evening Excursion (via Interpretive Bus/Van)

This is a late-afternoon and evening tour lasting (as previously mentioned) four to just over six hours depending on the departure location. Travel to the Northern Range including the Lamar Valley for exciting views of bears, elk, bison, wolves, pronghorn, and bighorn sheep. Departure locations are Canyon Village, Fishing Bridge RV Park, Lake Yellowstone Hotel, and the Bay Bridge Campground. This tour is operated via bus or van from mid-June through mid-August and via Historic Yellow Bus mid-August through mid-September. Tickets are $39 ($19.50) from Canyon Village and $46 (23) from the other three departure sites.

The Teton Vista Rendezvous Tour (via Historic Yellow Bus)

This all-day Historic Yellow Bus tour takes the visitor to see fabulous lakes, meadows, rugged mountains, and fantastic wildlife. If weather is not conducive to some of the sightseeing spots, stops at cultural sites or the Colter Bay Native Arts Museum will be substituted. Lunch will be at the Menor's Ferry area by the Snake River at Dornan's (cost not included). This tour departs from both the Old Faithful Inn as well as Grant Village from early June through mid-September. Plan on eight and a half hours from Grant Village and a full ten hours from the Old Faithful Inn. Tickets are $92 ($46).

The Yellowstone in a Day Tour (via Historic Yellow Bus)

This all-day tour lasts nearly ten hours and offers just what the name implies—a great overview of the entire park. This is basically the same tour described for bus or van but offered as a Historic Yellow Bus tour on Tuesdays and Saturdays departing from the Old Faithful Inn. Included is most every park highlight including Old Faithful, Yellowstone Lake, the Grand Canyon of the Yellowstone River, and much more. Lunch is not included in the ticket price. This tour is operated from early June through mid-September. Tickets are $92 ($46).

The Wake Up to Wildlife Tour (via Historic Yellow Bus)

This partial-day tour lasts four to just over five hours depending on departure location chosen. Early morning in the Lamar Valley is a great time to see abundant wildlife grazing and hunting. Continental breakfast and beverages are included in the ticket price. This tour is offered from Canyon Lodge, Mammoth Hotel, and Roosevelt Lodge. Cost is $75 ($37.50).

The Picture Perfect Photo Safari (via Historic Yellow Bus)

Like the above listed tour, this partial-day tour offers great opportunity to see and photograph wildlife in their natural habitat. The main difference is that this tour originates from southern parts of the park, specifically the Lake Yellowstone Hotel and the Old Faithful Inn. Continental breakfast is included. Running late May through late September, the cost is $81 ($40.50).

The Firehole Basin Adventure (via Historic Yellow Bus)
This just slightly more than "three-hour tour" will not risk shipwreck, but instead offers all four major geothermal features: geysers, hot springs, fumaroles, and mud pots. This tour is offered early June through early October and only from the Old Faithful Inn. Tickets are $46 ($23).

The Geyser Gazers Tour (via Historic Yellow Bus)
This is a relatively short adventure lasting just under two hours. This tour also departs from the Old Faithful Inn and travels the Grand Loop Road, taking in the sights of the Firehole Lake Drive. You'll see Firehole Spring, Great Fountain Geyser, Surprise Pool, and much more. The tour stops for a walk to see the many sites at the Midway Geyser Basin. This tour is offered early June through early September. Tickets are $25 ($12.50).

The Lake Butte Sunset Tour (via Historic Yellow Bus)
This is the first of three evening Historic Yellow Bus tours offered. This tour departs from the Lake Yellowstone Hotel and the Fishing Bridge RV Park. You'll enjoy sunset views of Yellowstone Lake and the Lake Butte Overlook. Lasting about two hours, this tour is offered early June through late September. The cost is $32 ($16).

The Evening Wildlife Encounters (via Historic Yellow Bus)
This Historic Yellow Bus evening tour provides a history lesson plus wildlife viewing at one of their most active times of the day with the top down on the bus. This is a three-hour tour originating from the Mammoth Hotel and the Canyon Lodge. It runs early June through mid September with a cost of $60 ($30).

108

The Twilight on the Firehole Tour (via Historic Yellow Bus)

This tour is brand new for 2010 and originates as an evening tour from the Old Faithful Inn lasting just over two hours. This tour provides views of this active thermal (or Firehole) section of the park at a time of day when the diminishing daylight gives it a unique golden glow. Wildlife is also more active at this time of day so have your camera ready. The cost is $32 ($16).

~

Xanterra Parks & Resorts provide much more in the way of activities than just tours. They also offer bike rental at the Old Faithful Snow Lodge with prices ranging from $35 for an adult bike ($22.50, child's bike) for a full day to $25 ($15) for a half day, to an hourly rate of $8 ($6). The bike shop is normally open June 1 through September 30 and can be reached at 307-545-4825.

~

There are one- and two-hour horseback trail rides available at Canyon Lodge, Roosevelt Lodge & Cabins, and the Mammoth Hot Springs Hotel. Riders must be at least eight years of age, four feet tall, and weigh no more than 240 pounds. Children eight–eleven years of age must be accompanied by an adult. Helmets are available on request.

Horses and stagecoach rides are the only two ways to get to the Yellowstone Old West Dinner Cookout (mentioned in chapter four under the Roosevelt Lodge dining options). Dinner here consists of steak (12 oz. serving for adults, 6 oz. for children), all you can eat sides including coleslaw, potato salad, baked beans, corn, corn muffins, watermelon, fruit crisp, and beverages. Options are a one-hour ride through sagebrush flats with a direct return or a two-hour ride with the addition of woods and meadows, also with a direct return. Each departure group accommodates twenty people. The Covered Wagon option takes thirty to forty-five minutes and goes through sagebrush flats. These are canvas wagons in groups of six wagons, each drawn by two horses, and holding up to thirty people.

Dinner is served in Pleasant Valley, a large meadow three miles from Roosevelt Lodge. Guests are seated together at picnic tables while the food is served buffet-style under a protective canvas roof. Entertainment, usually a cowboy singer is provided. For any of the Western Adventures, call the reservations office at 307-344-7311 or 1-866-GEYSERLAND (866-439-7375).

Xanterra also offers many differing water adventures. These include scenic cruises on Yellowstone Lake originating from the Bridge Bay Marina, outboard motorboat and rowboat rental, custom guided sightseeing or fishing tours, fly fishing guides, backcountry shuttle service, and more.

Yellowstone Lake scenic cruises are offered mid-June through mid-September, costing $14.25 for adults and $9 for children two through eleven years of age (children under the age of two are free). Custom guided sightseeing or fishing tours are offered as two-hour through twelve-hour options. Prices range from $152 to $1,152, depending on which of two boats (twenty-two foot or thirty-four foot) and tour length (2.0, 4.5, 7.0, 9.5, 12.0 hours). Prices include experienced fishing or sightseeing guides, fishing gear, life jackets, gas, and fish cleaning, if requested.

Boats available at the Bridge Bay Marina from mid-June through early September include sixteen-foot rowboats accommodating two–four people at $10.00/hour, $45/eight-hours, or $55.50/overnight. Eighteen-foot, 40-horsepower outboard motorboats accommodating two–six people are available for $47/hour.

Full-day fly fishing guides are available in advance by calling 307-344-5566 or by stopping by the front desk of any in-park lodging, based upon availability from early June through early October. The cost is $390 (one person), $418 (two people), $468 (three people), or $520 (four people). Price includes transportation to one of Yellowstone's well-known rivers or streams, lunch, soft drinks, and all flies. Full-day gear package including rod, reel, and waders is $26.50. You must have a valid Yellowstone National Park Fishing Permit (Wyoming state permit not required) if you are sixteen years of age or older. Permits are available at all ranger stations, visitor centers, General Stores, and the Xanterra Bridge Bay Marina at a cost of $15/three-day permit, $20/seven-day permit, and $35/season permit. Children under fifteen may fish without a permit if they are under the direct supervision of an adult with a valid permit; all children under the age of eighteen who fish must be accompanied by a responsible adult.

Finally, Backcountry Shuttle Service is available to get backpackers in groups of up to six, from the Bay Bridge Marina to the drop off points of Eagle Bay, Wolf Bay, Plover Point, Promontory, or Columbine Creek.

For Backcountry Shuttle hours, information, and reservations, call the Backcountry Shuttle Office at 307-242-3893. For more information on any of the other services listed in this chapter call 866-GEYSERLAND (866-439-7375) or 307-344-7311.

~

Winter activities provided by Xanterra Parks & Resorts are far too numerous to list in full detail here. At their Web site, I counted twelve different snowcoach routes offered ranging from $32.75 to $150; five ski and snowshoe tours ranging from $25 to $140; two evening programs, express trips between West Yellowstone and Old Faithful, for $52; and Interpretive Bus Tours. For complete and up-to-date details of these activities, including pricing, locations, and times, go to www.nps.gov/yell/planyourvisit/concessnprog.htm.

Also, while I have listed many of the Xanterra offerings, they are just one of a large number of transportation and winter service providers permitted to operate within Yellowstone National Park. I counted sixty-four permitted transportation providers and fifty-one winter service providers. At last count, there are fifteen snowcoach providers (mostly from the south and west entrances), twenty-three snowmobile providers (again, mostly from the south and west entrances), and thirteen cross-country skiing operators. For complete and up-to-date listings, visit www.nps.gov/yell/planyourvisit/transbusn.htm for permitted transportation providers, and www.nps.gov/yell/planyourvisit/wintbusn.htm for permitted winter service providers.

Chapter 9

IMPORTANT PHONE NUMBERS AND WEB SITES

YELLOWSTONE NATIONAL PARK

EMERGENCY   911

Mammoth Medical Clinic
   (open year-round)   307-344-7965

Old Faithful Medical Clinic   307-545-7325
                                      (intermittent winter
                                      hours – call Mammoth at
                                      307-344-7965 for winter
                                      appointments)

Lake Medical Clinic (closed
   in winter)   307-242-7241

General Park Information   307-344-7381
     Option 1 – lodging
     Option 3 – camping
     Option 4 – information packet

Option 5 – weather/road
   conditions
Option 6 – fees/backcountry use
Option 7 – employment   www.nps.gov/yell

Visitor's Guide to Accessible
   Features   307-344-2386 (TDD)
                                  www.nps.gov/yell/
                                  planyourvisit/parkwide-
                                  access.htm

Reservations for lodging, dining,
   camping, boating, and other
   activities
      (Dinner reservations are
   required for the Grant Village
   Dining Room, the Lake
   Yellowstone Hotel Dining
   Room, the Old Faithful Inn
   Dining Room, the Mammoth
   Hotel Dining Room (winter
   season only), the Old Faithful
   Snow Lodge Obsidian Dining
   Room (winter season only)
   and for the Old West
   Dinner Cookouts)   307-344-7311
                                  307-344-5395 TDD
                                  866-439-7375 TDD
                                  toll-free
www.yellowstonenationalparklodges.com/lodging-71.html
www.yellowstonenationalparklodges.com/Dining-76.html
www.yellowstonenationalparklodges.com/Yellowstone-
   Activities-Search-7168.html

Yellowstone National
    Park Lodges   Xanterra Parks & Resorts
                                   P.O. Box 165
                                   Yellowstone NP, WY 82190

Camping   Xanterra Parks & Resorts
                                   P.O. Box 165
                                   Yellowstone NP, WY 82190
                                   307-344-7311 or 307-344-
                                   7901 (same-day reserve)
                                   866-GEYSERLAND (future
                                   reserve)
                                   866-439-7375 (future
                                   reserve)
                                   www.travelyellowstone.
                                   com

Group Camping (Madison,
    Grant, and Bridge Bay)   Xanterra Parks & Resorts
                                   P.O. Box 165
                                   Yellowstone NP, WY 82190
                                   307-344-7311
                                   866-GEYSERLAND
                                   866-439-7375
                                   e-mail YNPSA@Xanterra.
                                   com

Park Crime Reporting
    Tip Line   307-344-2132

Road Conditions   307-344-2117

National Weather Service
for both Yellowstone
and Grand Teton   www.crh.noaa.gov/
                               riw/?n=ynp_gtnp

WYDOT road information   888-WYO-ROAD or
                               www.wyoroad.info/

MTDOT road information   406-444-6200 or www.
                               mdt.mt.gov/travinfo/

Tours (sightseeing)   Xanterra Parks & Resorts
                               P.O. Box 165
                               Yellowstone NP, WY
                               82190
                               866-GEYSERLAND
                               866-439-7375 or
                               307-344-7311
www.yellowstonenationalparklodges.com/summer-tours-
     activities-256.html
or www.yellowstonenationalparklodges.com/Interpretive-
     Tours-256_1362.html

Tours (certified guides and
     outfitters)   307-344-7381
www.yellowstonenationalparklodges.com/Interpretive-
     Tours-256_1362.html

Hiking (trail maps
     and descriptions)   www.nps.gov/yell/
                               planyourvisit/hiking.htm

Horseback Riding	Xanterra Parks & Resorts P.O. Box 165 Yellowstone NP, WY 82190 307-344-7311 or 866-439-7375 307-344-5395 (TDD) 307-344-2160 (backcountry trips with stock) www.nps.gov/yell/planyourvisit/horseride.htm Yellowstone Wilderness Outfitters P.O. Box 745 Yellowstone NP, WY 82190 406-223-3300 www.yellowstone.ws
Stables (boarding outside the park)	North Yellowstone Stables Gardiner, MT 406-223-7845
Kennel options outside the park	www.nps.gov/yell/planyourvisit/kennels.htm
Bike Rental (Old Faithful Snow Lodge)	307-545-4825

Albright Visitor Center, Mammoth
(open year-round except
Veterans Day and
Thanksgiving Day)   307-344-2263
8:00 a.m. – 7:00 p.m.,
summer season
9:00 a.m. – 5:00 p.m.,
winter season

Canyon Visitor Education Center   307-344-2550
8:00 a.m. – 8:00 p.m.,
peak season
Reduced hours, early
and late season

Fishing Bridge Visitor Center   307-344-2450
8:00 a.m. – 7:00 p.m.,
peak season
Reduced hours, early
and late season

Grant Village Visitor Center   307-344-2650
8:00 a.m. – 7:00 p.m.,
peak season
Reduced hours, early
and late season

Madison Information Center   307-344-2821
9:00 a.m. – 6:00 p.m.,
peak season

Norris Geyser Basin Museum &
  Information Station   307-344-2812
                             9:00 a.m. – 6:00 p.m., peak
                             season

Old Faithful Visitor Education
  Center   307-344-2750
                             8:00 a.m. – 7:00 p.m., peak
                             season
                             8:00 a.m. – 8:00 p.m.,
                             information window
                             Reduced hours, early and
                             late season
                             Reopens mid-December for
                             winter

Old Faithful Eruption
  Predictions   307-344-2751, dial 1

West Yellowstone Visitor
  Information Center   307-344-2876
                             8:00 a.m. – 8:00 p.m., peak
                             season
                             Reduced hours, early and
                             late season

Park Accessibility
  Coordinator   P.O. Box 168
                             Yellowstone NP, WY 82190
                             307-344-2386 (TDD only)
                             www.nps.gov/yell/
                             planyourvisit

Sign Language Interpreters	307-344-2581
To report the release of fish, plants, or animals into a body of water they did not originate in:	307-344-7381, dial 0
Overnight Backpacking Permits	Backcountry Office P.O. Box 168 Yellowstone NP, WY 82190
Backcountry Shuttle Office	307-242-3893
Yellowstone Association Institute	406-848-2400 www.Yellowstone Association.org www.nps.gov/yell/ forteachers (field classes for teachers)
Yellowstone Park Foundation	222 East Main Street, Suite 301 Bozeman, MT 59715 406-586-6303 www.ypf.org
Lost & Found (lodging areas) (other areas)	307-344-5387 307-344-2107

120

Service Stations at Canyon
    Village, Fishing Bridge,
    Grant Village, Old Faithful
    (gas, diesel, wreckers,
    and repair)   406-848-7548

Area Chambers of Commerce

    MONTANA
    Big Sky   406-995-3000
    Billings   800-735-2635
    Bozeman   800-228-4224
    Cooke City/Silver Gate   406-838-2495
    Gardiner   406-848-7971
    Livingston   406-222-0850
    Red Lodge   888-281-0625
    W. Yellowstone   406-646-7701

    WYOMING
    Cody   800-393-2639
    Dubois   307-455-2556
    East Yellowstone/Wapiti
        Valley   307-587-9595
    Jackson   307-733-3316

    IDAHO
    Idaho Falls   866-365-6943
    Eastern Idaho Visitor
        Information Center   800-634-3246

Lodging outside the park:

West Yellowstone Chamber
of Commerce

30 Yellowstone Avenue or
P.O. Box 458
West Yellowstone, MT
59758
406-646-7701 (phone)
406-646-9691 (fax)
www.destinationyellow
stone.com
e-mail: visitorservices@
westyellowstonechamber.
com

Gardiner Chamber of
Commerce

222 W. Park Street or P.O.
Box 81
Gardiner, MT 59030
406-848-7971 (phone)
406-848-2446 (fax)
www.gardinerchamber.
com
e-mail: info@
gardinerchamber.com

Cody County Chamber
of Commerce

836 Sheridan Avenue
Cody, WY 82414-3411
307-587-2777 and
307-587-2297
www.codychamber.org

Cooke City/Silver Gate Chamber
of Commerce 109 West Main Street or
P.O. Box 1071
Cooke City, MT 59020
406-838-2495
www.cookecitychamber.
org
e-mail: info@
cookecitychamber.org

Mammoth Chapel 307-344-2003
Superintendent's Office
www.yellowstone
ministry.org/worship-
service-schedule/

GRAND TETON NATIONAL PARK

EMERGENCY 911

Medical Clinic (near Jackson
Lake Lodge, mid-May to
early October) 307-543-2514
307-733-8002 (after hours)

General Park Information
(camping, lodging,
backcountry and climbing
information, or direct
contact to a visitor center) 307-739-3300, dial 1
www.nps.gov/grte

Overnight Lodging (within
 the park)   307-739-3603, dial 1

Overnight Camping (within
 the park)   307-739-3603, dial 2

Weather Information   307-739-3611

Road Conditions   307-739-3682

<u>Lodging (direct lines listed below)</u>

Jackson Hole Chamber of
 Commerce   114 Center Street or
            P.O. Box 550
            Jackson, WY 83001
            307-733-3316
            www.jacksonhole
            chamber.com
            e-mail: info@
            jacksonhole
            chamber.com

Colter Bay Cabins (opens
 late May)   800-628-9988

Colter Bay RV Park (opens
 late May)
            800-628-9988

Dornan's Spur Ranch Cabins
   (open year-round)   307-733-2522

Flagg Ranch Resort (opens
   late May)   307-543-2861 or
                                        800-443-2311

Jackson Lake Lodge (opens
   mid-May)   800-628-9988

Jenny Lake Lodge (opens
   late May)   307-733-4647

Signal Mt. Lodge (opens
   early May)   800-672-6012

Campgrounds (direct lines listed below - maximum stay
is 7 days at Jenny Lake, 14 days at all other campgrounds,
30 days total per year)

Colter Bay Campground (late
   May to late September)
   350 individual, 9 walk-in,
   11 group
   filling time: rarely fills   800-628-9988

Colter Bay Tent Village Park
   (late May to late August)
   66 tent cabin sites
   filling time: call for information 800-628-9988

Colter Bay RV Park (late May to
    late September)
    112 RV sites, RV hookups
    filling time: call for information 800-628-9988

Flagg Ranch Campground (mid/late
    May to mid/late September)
    158 sites (74 tent, 84 RV),
    RV hookups
    filling time: call for information 800-443-2311

Gros Ventre Campground (early
    May to early October)
    350 individual sites, 5 group   800-628-9988,
    filling time: rarely fills   direct 307-734-4431

Jenny Lake Campground
    (mid-May to late September)
    tents only, 49 individual sites,
    10 walk-in sites
    filling time: 11:00 a.m.   800-628-9988

Lizard Creek Campground (early
    June to end of August)
    60 individual sites,
    30-foot veh. max.
    filling time: rarely fills   800-672-6012

Signal Mountain Campground
    (early May to mid-October)
    86 individual sites, 1 RV
    hookup site, 30-foot veh. max.
    filling time: mid-afternoon   800-672-6012

Visitor Centers

Colter Bay Visitor Center &
    Indian Arts Museum
       307-739-3594
       early May
       – mid-October

Flagg Ranch Information Station
       307-543-2372
       early June – early
       September

Jenny Lake Ranger Station
    (climbing information)
       307-739-3343
       late May –
       mid-September

Jenny Lake Visitor Center
       307-739-3392
       mid-May – late
       September

Craig Thomas Visitor Center
       307-739-3399
       open year-round

Laurance S. Rockefeller Preserve
    Center
       307-739-3654
       late May – late
       September

Chapter 10

WHY IS A NATIONAL PARK VACATION ECONOMICAL?

J ust in case you always thought of the national parks as an expensive trip or a vacation for the rich and famous, you will be pleased to learn that this is not the case. Let's get the expensive part out of the way first.

Unless you are one of the lucky ones who live within a reasonable drive of a major national park like Yellowstone, you will have to purchase airfare and a rental car at the airport. These items are expensive; I agree. However, this is where the expensive part ends. Remember, as I stated earlier, your admission to the park is $25 (and remember, it's valid at both Yellowstone NP and Grand Teton NP). That's all, for an entire week, and for your entire family. Oh sure, you can stay in the most expensive lodging and eat at the most expensive restaurants in the national parks, but you don't have to as you have other options as well!

Get out your calculator and start adding the cost for admission to a theme park, sporting event, etc. Be sure to budget for each member of your family and for each day. Getting kind of expensive, isn't it? Now add in food.

Again, if you are a hiker, you are talking sub sandwiches with Subway® type prices for lunch on the trail every day. Breakfast can be muffins and fruit from the grocery.

Oh, did I forget lodging? Book early, preferably a year in advance if you know what you wish to do because the demand for a room within the boundaries of Yellowstone far exceeds the supply. Prices for standard rooms are reasonable and vary from a high of $231 to $122 at the Old Faithful Inn or $219 to $145 at the Lake Yellowstone Hotel, to a low of $117 for a room with a private bath or $87 for a room with shared bathroom facilities at the Mammoth Hot Springs Hotel. Cabins range from a high of $213 for a Hot Tub Cabin at the Mammoth Hot Springs Hotel and Cabins to a low of $66 for a Budget Cabin at the Old Faithful Lodge Cabins or $65 for a Roughrider Cabin at the Roosevelt Lodge Cabins. If you want to spend more for luxury, yes, it's available too, even in a national park. Suite options include $545 for the Presidential Suite at the Lake Yellowstone Hotel, $502 for a suite at the Old Faithful Inn, and $439 for a suite at the Mammoth Hot Springs Hotel. Basic rule of thumb: accommodations with a private bathroom go first and fast. Compare these prices to what you normally spend for a room at a typical chain hotel along some highway you soon forgot, or at any hotel downtown any major U.S. city!

Then there's the evening entertainment. Remember, there's a fantastic and free ranger program. Compare that to Cirque Du Soleil® ticket prices, a big-league baseball game, or a Broadway show. Getting the picture? Other than getting there, this is the most economical way I can think of to spend a high-quality week with your family.

Chapter 11

WILDLIFE IN YELLOWSTONE

The Yellowstone–Grand Teton area is often rated the very best of all the U.S. national parks for wildlife sighting. The National Park Service states that Yellowstone is home to the largest concentration of mammals in the continental United States with sixty-seven mammals calling it home. Mammals abundant in Yellowstone include both grizzly and black bear, moose, wolves, coyote, elk, bison, bighorn sheep, mountain lion, bobcat, wolverine, lynx, beaver, and more. Also present are multiple amphibians including blotched tiger salamander, boreal chorus frog, Columbia spotted frog, and the boreal toad, multiple reptiles including bull snake, prairie rattlesnake, valley garter snake, wandering garter snake, rubber boa, and the sagebrush lizard. Bird species found in Yellowstone include bald eagle, whooping crane, trumpeter swan, harlequin duck, common loon, osprey, peregrine falcon, and many more. Official Yellowstone NP statistics estimate the park is home to approximately one hundred grizzly bear, one hundred twenty gray wolves, fourteen to twenty-three cougar, twenty thousand elk (in summer), twenty-three hundred to twenty-five hundred mule deer, thirty-three hundred bison, two hundred fifty to two hundred seventy-five bighorn sheep, one hundred seventy-five to two hundred twenty-five mountain goats, and two hundred pronghorns. Referred to simply as "common" are black bear, coyote, fox, bobcat, badger, and many more. Remember to stay at least one hundred yards away from bears and wolves and at least twenty-five yards away from all other animals. Always ask park officials about both weather conditions and wildlife sightings. The wildlife at Yellowstone or any national park is not to be feared; however, wildlife must be respected, understood, and given plenty of space.

I have visited most of the great national parks in the United States and western Canada and have never had a bad or even close to dangerous experience with wildlife. First of all, even though the National Park Service records show 2,239 bear sightings reported in Yellowstone in 2007, with multiple trips to the park, I have never seen a single bear at Yellowstone. Now, don't let this give you a false and potentially deadly sense of security that you will not; it just means that you should not expect to be seeing bears everywhere you go like you do fish in tanks at a pet store. I have seen plenty of bear, both black and grizzly at numerous national parks including Glacier, Yosemite, Kings Canyon, Denali, plus Jasper and Banff National Parks in Canada. Then again, you just never know and this is where the danger lies. I took five trips to Yosemite before seeing black bear there and when I did, I saw three in one day. The 2,239 reported sightings in 2007 at Yellowstone break down as 1,527 grizzly bear, 673 black bear, and 39 where the species could not be determined. While you do not want to tangle with either species of bear, grizzly bears are much more aggressive than black bear. Also, know that black bear is a species, and not necessarily descriptive of the color. They may be golden, cinnamon, brown, or black in color. In any case, do not let the knowledge that there is wildlife running wild in a national park keep you from enjoying the park.

While you should never attempt to touch or even approach any wild animal (remember the rules - stay at least one hundred yards away from bears and wolves and at least twenty-five yards away from all other animals), most wildlife will not even consider approaching humans, as long as you mind your business and let them go about theirs. Remember, this is their home, and you are the visitor here.

A park ranger at Jasper National Park in Alberta Canada once told the audience at a program I was attending, that there was greater chance of getting killed by falling trees than by a bear. Most of Yellowstone's wildlife will not pose any threat to you under normal conditions; however, exceptions include bears, bison, mountain lions, and poisonous snakes such as rattlesnakes. Even wolves and coyotes will not normally approach humans, unless it is a very small child left wandering alone. Be sure to keep small children close, especially on trails, and be prepared to pick them up. Both rattlesnakes and mountain lions are usually calm, quiet, and very elusive. Rattlesnakes make a hissing-type sound. Their sound might also be described as similar to a baby's rattle; hence the name. Experts say rattlesnakes will not attack unless cornered or disturbed. However, they are known to defend themselves. If you see one, keep your distance.

Bears are much the same and will probably not be seen if you make noise. When hiking or where your sight line might be impaired by trees or brush, especially if you might be downwind from an animal on trails, talk to yourself or others in your party, sing, carry a "bear bell," clap your hands, or loudly say, "Hello, bear." If the animal knows you are nearing, it will instinctively go in another direction. These animals will attack you only if they feel threatened, cornered, have young with them, believe you want to harm them or their young, or do not know you are there until you are right upon them. I have hiked in every park I've visited, including all over Glacier National Park, where the "WARNING BEAR COUNTRY" signs are posted everywhere.

Some people think I am a nerd, probably for more reasons than just the fact that I wear a bell, but it never hurts. It cost me $3.99 at a souvenir shop, many years ago, at Glacier National Park. I always look like the "dork" with my "bear bell." Be advised that there are some conflicting studies as to the effectiveness of bear bells. I hum, sing, and talk to myself or others in my party, and have never had a problem. However, on the rare incidence where you see a bear, it is important to know how to react.

If you find yourself too close to a grizzly bear, black bear, or mountain lion, make yourself bigger, and do not run (bears can easily outrun you) or panic. Do not drop your backpack. Do not climb a tree (they will climb up after you). Hold your arms up, stand tall, put children on your shoulders, and stand close together with others in your party. However, do not surround the animal; leave it a way to get away from you. Again, it should be expected to attack only if it feels cornered. The animal will see you as more intimidating and larger and will be less likely to think it can attack you and win the fight. Speak calmly to the bear, tell it to get away and back off slowly.

Bears may bluff charge humans. If this happens, stand your ground, continue to make yourself look as large as you can, and let the bear back off. Then you should immediately do the same. Actual bear attacks are very rare. However, if indeed, despite all this, you are attacked, some bear experts suggest curling up in a ball on the ground with your hands covering the back of your neck; this position will protect two of your most vulnerable areas, your stomach and your neck. Others say to lie completely flat on the ground on your stomach with your legs slightly spread and clasp your hands over the back of your neck (this is the advice I received at Yellowstone). With either option, bear experts usually say to be courageous enough to remain silent and lie still; however, if you are attacked at night or if you feel you are being attacked as prey, most say to fight back with all you've got to let the bear know you are not easy prey.

If you can "bear" the facts (get it?), here are some: The National Park Service, Department of the Interior statistics, show that from 1980 through 2002, with over sixty-two million people visiting Yellowstone NP, there were thirty-two people injured by bears. They put the chance of being injured by a bear at one in 1.9 million. Another way I like to look at it is thirty-two incidents in twenty-three years is about 1.5 per year with an average of about 2.7 million visitors per year during this period. Human injuries have decreased from an average of forty-eight per year in the 1930s, '40s, '50s, and '60s, to less than one per year in the 2000s. This is due to many things including better educating first the parks and park personnel, and then, in turn, the park visitors on what to do and what not to do around bears. In the earlier part of the twentieth century, many national parks used to advertise bear viewings at poorly stored garbage areas.

Historically, the vast majority of injuries have been due to people getting too close to bears to take pictures or even attempting to hand feed the bears. With drastic changes to the way garbage is stored, rules against getting within one hundred yards of a bear, rules on (and an understanding of) how to store food if camping or hiking, plus regulations on the storage of food in vehicles parked overnight, as you can see, incidents have been dramatically reduced. Again, with over sixty-two million visitors in just the 1980 through 2002 period alone, estimating all time total visitations at Yellowstone would be impossible. However, conservatively placing it in the hundreds of millions, it is amazing that there have been just six documented bear-caused human fatalities and one more possible fatality. Unfortunately, one of these fatalities was very recent when an Illinois man ignored warning signs posted advising hikers to avoid an area near the east entrance to the park; this occurred on June 17, 2010. Prior to this unfortunate event, twenty-four years had passed since the last bear-caused human fatality which occurred in 1986 when a photographer approached an adult female grizzly bear too closely in Hayden Valley. Again, heed these statistics, be careful, know how to behave if you do see a bear, but go on and enjoy your vacation in this fantastic place called Yellowstone. Current management policies on bears have reduced drastically not only human injuries but also property damage claims from two hundred nineteen per year in the 1960s to about fifteen per year in the 2000s. The number of bears having to be killed or removed from the park has decreased from thirty-three black and four grizzlies per year in the 1960s to an average of one black bear and one grizzly bear every three years in the 2000s. Bear relocations are also way down from more than fifty grizzlies and one hundred black bear per year in the 1960s to just under a half black and just over a half grizzly per year in the 2000s.

The bottom line here is that you must be "bear smart." Bears want nothing to do with humans. For example, if you are hiking down a trail near a bear and they hear or smell you coming, they will go another direction and you will never even know they were there. Remember what they say, "You do not have to be able to outrun the bears, just the other campers!" Think about it!

Proper food storage is critical. Remember that bears can be anywhere in the park and at any time. You must keep food items locked in your car or in a bear box. Park regulations require campers to store food in approved bear-proof food canisters while backpacking below ten thousand feet. All food, food containers, and utensils must be stored in a bear box or hidden in a closed and locked vehicle with the windows rolled up except during the transport, preparation, or consumption of food. Garbage must be stored in the same manner as food, or placed in bear-resistant trash cans. Remember that any item with a fragrant smell, including soap, lotions, toothpaste, and perfumes/colognes should be considered food for bears and treated in the same manner as food. No food, food containers, or garbage may be stored in tents or sleeping bags. Ice chests, thermoses, water containers, grills, dishes, etc. must be stored in the same manner as actual food; hidden inside a locked vehicle or bear box. Never abandon food because of an approaching bear; take it with you. Never throw your backpack or food at a bear to distract it. Do not drop your backpack as it can protect your back if attacked. Never bury food scraps, grease, or fish remains, and never leave food, food containers, or garbage unattended in camp.

Bison Near the Old Faithful Inn

Bison (often called buffalo) are the largest of all the mammals in Yellowstone. They are strictly vegetarian, weigh up to eighteen hundred pounds (males or bulls) or one thousand pounds (females or cows), and stand six feet tall at the shoulder. Bison are surprisingly fast and can run at speeds more than thirty miles per hour. Males are often less tolerant of human activity than females. Yellowstone NP is the only place in the continental United States where they have persisted without interruption since prehistoric times. The population dwindled to fewer than fifty in 1902, but due to policy changes and aggressively bringing in additional bison from nearby herds the population grew to an estimate of today's population at somewhere between three thousand to four thousand animals. They are often seen grazing in open meadow or along river valleys, although, every time I have been to Yellowstone, they are always just outside the Old Faithful Inn and geyser area as well. Keep your distance (at least twenty-five yards)

and know that more people are hurt by bison each year at Yellowstone than by bears!

A major issue concerning Yellowstone bison is a disease named brucellosis, a condition that can cause bison and domestic cattle to abort their first calf. Approximately half of Yellowstone's bison test positive for brucellosis (as do much of Yellowstone's elk). It is believed the first bison probably contracted the disease from cattle raised in the park as a source of meat and milk for park visitors in the early 1900s. There is no cure for brucellosis.

Wolves, once very common in Yellowstone NP and the greater Yellowstone area, became former residents of the area after the last pack was intentionally killed off in 1926. After years of debate and discussion, and with the assistance of the protection provided by the Endangered Species Act of 1973, gray wolves were reintroduced to the area in January of 1995. While the wolf has been removed from the federal endangered species list, put back on, then removed once again, etc., today their numbers are estimated at more than four hundred in the greater Yellowstone area; more than one hundred live in the park itself. The wolves of Yellowstone live about three to four years, weigh up to 110 pounds (female) or 130 pounds (male), and may be gray, black, or rarely white. Do not expect to see one, and consider yourself very lucky if you do. Remember to stay at least one hundred yards away from wolves and bears.

Finally, a word on the wildlife that is probably the most important to you—your pets. My advice—LEAVE THEM AT HOME! This is far too large a wilderness, with terribly cold nights much of the year and abundant dangerous large mammals to risk harm to your Schnauzer. What do you plan to do with Fido while you embark on a strenuous all-day hike? I listed the link for kennels just outside the park in chapter nine if you regularly travel with your pets and want to board them while at Yellowstone. There are no kennel accommodations actually in the park. However, here is a short summary of the National Park Service's published regulations regarding pets at Yellowstone.

1) Pets are prohibited in the backcountry and on trails and boardwalks for many reasons. Visitors should not have their park experience interrupted by other people's pets; domestic animals generally lack the ability to survive in the wild. A loose dog could lead a bear right back to you. Your pet could easily become prey. Thermal areas pose a great threat to your pets (they are not particularly good at reading the warning signs!). Dogs, in particular, do not seem to recognize any difference between cold and hot water. Dogs have died horrible deaths diving into scalding hot springs!

2) Pets may accompany you in the front country areas of the park if under physical control at all times: leashed (six foot or less), crated, or caged. This includes areas within one hundred feet of roads, parking areas, and campgrounds.

3) It is against park regulations to leave a pet unattended and tied to an object.

4) Pets, like humans, should leave no traces other than footprints. You must clean up and properly dispose of all pet feces!

Chapter 12

WHAT TO DO IF YOU HAVE ONLY ONE, TWO, OR THREE DAYS

The first thing to do if you only have one day to spend at this magical park is to sit down and have a good cry, pound the dash of your car, or look in the mirror and get really mad at yourself for not dedicating more time to your trip. Yellowstone necessitates and deserves much more than one day to do it justice. I would compare this situation to taking your kids to Disney World for the first time and telling them after you enter the gate that they only have ten minutes to do it all.

Oh well, if you do indeed have just ONE DAY at Yellowstone for your first visit, I would concentrate on the geyser/geothermal areas between Madison Junction and Old Faithful. The Old Faithful Geyser is the most famous feature at Yellowstone. Right next to the Geyser is the unbelievable Old Faithful Inn. Here you can enjoy the monstrous lobby of this fabulous rustic lodge, taking in all its grandeur and history. They simply do not build anything this magnificent today. You can have a meal at the inn and spend the afternoon touring the varied and numerous geyser basins, pools, mud pots, steam vents, and hot springs in the area. If you plan well, get an early start, and commit to sticking to your plans, you could travel farther east for lunch in the West Thumb and Grant Village areas where you can get great views of Yellowstone Lake, then have dinner at the Old Faithful Inn and take in the evening ranger program at Old Faithful.

If you have only TWO DAYS, I would add to the above two half-day side trips to any two of the following: the Grand Canyon of the Yellowstone River featuring the Lower Falls of the Yellowstone River, Mammoth Hot Springs, the Lake and Fishing Bridge area for better exposure to Yellowstone Lake including visiting the beautiful Lake Yellowstone Hotel, or a decent hike.

If you are fortunate enough to have THREE DAYS, then your possibilities are far less limited. While you can spend weeks and months at Yellowstone, three days will give you a fairly broad experience. Rather than be forced to pick and choose, you could take in all four half-day suggestions above, or take in my favorite activity at any national park, a full-day exhaustive hike. Of course, there are many other options with three days or more including biking, fishing, horseback riding, ranger programs, photography, boating, historic buildings, visitor center activities, and more. My suggestion, better make that my strong suggestion to be exact, is to plan at least a week or more and plan to spend at least a day or two of your vacation at Grand Teton National Park just to the south. You've come a long way from home; don't regret not allocating sufficient time!

Whatever you do, do not miss the historic Old Faithful Inn. This will be one of the most magnificent and interesting structures you will ever walk into in your entire lifetime; plan to visit around mealtime and experience eating in this fantastic surrounding. Do not miss Old Faithful Geyser. It may not even be the best geyser, but it definitely is the most famous and the poster child for Yellowstone National Park. Also, be sure to take in at least one evening ranger program. These programs are always well done, and are given by a fantastically knowledgeable park ranger in a very relaxing end-of-day format. They are fun for both adults and children, and are absolutely free.

Chapter 13

ACTIVITIES JUST FOR THE KIDS

National parks, including Yellowstone, are great places for kids to have fun. They will enjoy the various wildlife, old-fashioned campfires, interpretive displays at the visitor centers, and much more. One of the great things about a national park vacation is that much of the activity is truly "fun for the entire family" with activities like short easy hikes, bike rental, water activities, wildlife watching, etc. However, every major national park including Yellowstone offers activities designed especially with your younger family members in mind. It is best to check the free park newspaper, *Yellowstone Today*, or ask a ranger at any visitor center for specifics.

The best activity for kids, in my opinion, is the Junior Ranger Program for kids five to twelve years of age. A self-guided twelve-page activity booklet costs $3 at the various visitor centers throughout the park. Children must complete the booklet, requiring them to participate in various activities including attending a ranger-led program; hiking a park trail; completing various paper activities on park resources and issues; and showing an understanding of various concepts including geothermal geology, park wildlife, and fire ecology. Upon completion, and after reviewing their work with a park ranger, your child will be so proud and excited to be named a Junior Ranger, sworn in with an oath by a park ranger. They will receive a nice-looking official Yellowstone Junior Ranger patch (some parks award plastic badges while others, like Yellowstone, award patches). Summer patches feature a bear track for children eight–twelve years of age, and a wolf track for younger kids five–seven years of age. Five- to seven-year-olds must attend a ranger program, hike a trail, know why rules are important, complete the sentence "I want to be a Junior Ranger because…," be able to locate Yellowstone NP on a map, and point out the roads they and their family have traveled within the park. They must also complete their choice of four of seven other options on the topics of geysers, wildlife, plant life, and habitats. The program for eight- to twelve-year-olds requires attending a ranger program, visiting a visitor center and explaining what they learned, hiking a park trail, reading and understanding the Junior Ranger Pledge, understanding park rules, answering questions on Yellowstone, plus choosing four activities from a list of ten options if eight–nine years old and six of the ten if ten–twelve years old. The list includes activities on the Yellowstone ecosystem; habitats; identifying animals from their tracks; understanding basic information on black and grizzly bear; wildfires; and geothermal functions including geysers, hot springs, mud pots, and fumaroles. There is a winter-specific program offered for winter-season visitors with the child receiving a snowflake patch. Be advised that the winter Junior Ranger program requires the use of a thermometer and hand lens (available in a "snowpack") and snowshoes. Snowpacks are available at both Mammoth and Old Faithful visitor centers, while snowshoes may be checked out at Mammoth. Yellowstone swears in approximately twenty thousand Junior Rangers each year. My children are too old now, but through the years, they both became Junior Rangers at Denali, Grand Canyon, Yellowstone, Grand Teton, Crater Lake, Oregon Caves, Kenai Fjords, Redwood, and other national parks and national monuments.

Junior Ranger – Yellowstone NP
Young Naturalist – Grand Teton NP

For ages five to adult, Yellowstone offers the Young Scientist program. A self-guided booklet is available for $5 at either the Canyon Visitor Education Center or the Old Faithful Visitor Education Center. Participants must complete activities that investigate the mysteries of the park. Programs are offered for three distinct age groups: five–nine, ten–thirteen, and fourteen and up. The program for five- to nine-year-olds is offered only at Old Faithful. The Old Faithful programs require one to check out a Young Scientist Toolkit that includes a thermometer, stopwatch, and more. Those who complete the program receive an official Young Scientist patch or key chain. The park swears, in approximately eighteen hundred Young Scientists annually.

Additionally, Yellowstone offers many fun on-line activities for children as well. These include animal alphabet books, coloring book pages, scavenger hunts, knowledge quizzes, puzzles, and word games. You may find these of most benefit prior to your trip to get the entire family excited about the trip, just in case your kids think amusement parks are the only way to vacation! There are even resources for teachers including electronic field trips and educational programs at "Windows into Wonderland" or under "Expedition: Yellowstone!" pages. Check out all these activities out at www.nps.gov/yell/forkids/index.htm.

Finally, there is a four-day, family package of learning, adventure, and activity offered by the Yellowstone Association Institute. Family activities include animal tracking, wildlife watching photography, daily hiking, and much more. The package is designed for families with children between the ages of eight and twelve. It includes four nights of lodging at Mammoth Hot Springs Hotel or Grant Village, four breakfasts and lunches per person, naturalist guides, transportation for field trips, and evening programs with the National Park Service and Yosemite National Park Lodges. For complete details, call 307-344-5566.

Chapter 14

WEATHER, WINTER, ROAD CLOSURES, AND SNOW CHAIN REQUIREMENTS

Weather, much like the black or grizzly bear, is not a reason to avoid coming to Yellowstone. It is yet another good reason to come. However, weather is something to pay close attention to; always know what is forecast for the days to come.

Temperatures vary greatly by elevation, and therefore, by sections of the park. While summer daytime temperatures are often in the seventies and occasionally the eighties, the nights are still cool and may drop below freezing at higher elevations. Thunderstorms are common during the afternoon periods. Spring and fall daytime highs range from the thirties to the sixties with nighttime lows often in the teens or even single digits. Snow is common in the spring and fall with regular accumulations of up to a foot in a twenty-four-hour period. However, winter is another thing all to itself. This may be one of the most beautiful places in the entire country but it is also often one of the coldest. Daylight hours often stay anywhere between zero and the twenties; nighttime is regularly well below zero with the record low at -66 Fahrenheit. Snow accumulations average about 150 inches per year and the higher elevations often get twice that much.

As previously stated, only two roads are plowed for wheeled vehicles in winter, mid-December until sometime in March. Mainly the northern road from the North Entrance down to Mammoth and east through the Northeast Entrance is open. Also, the half mile of road from Mammoth Hot Springs to the parking area at the Upper Terraces is plowed. They are maintained only during daylight hours and may be suddenly closed during severe winter storms. Be prepared for snowpack, ice, and large drifts. Snow tires or tire chains may be required and are always recommended and a good idea. The speed limit for all vehicles is 45 mph, or lower where posted.

Winter opening dates for oversnow vehicles are approximately the following:

- Mid-December for most roads

- Mid to late December for the road between the East Entrance and Fishing Bridge

Oversnow travel closing dates are approximately the following:

- March 1 for the road from the East Entrance to Lake Butte (Sylvan Pass)

- Early March for Mammoth to Norris and Madison to Norris to Canyon

- Early to mid-March for Canyon to Fishing Bridge

- Mid-March for all other groomed roads to close

Only approved commercially guided oversnow vehicles are allowed on other park roads. The park is open for oversnow vehicles from 7:00 a.m. to 9:00 p.m. (East Entrance opens at 8:00 a.m.).

Spring road openings are listed below. Remember that the North Entrance to the Northeast Entrance at Silver Gate and Cooke City, Montana, is open year-round. The rest of the park roads will open on the approximate dates listed to wheeled vehicles. Once each road opens, it is open twenty-four hours a day.

- Mid-April for Mammoth to Norris Junction to Madison Junction; the West Entrance to Madison Junction to Old Faithful; Norris Junction to Canyon

- Early May for Canyon to Fishing Bridge/Lake to the East Entrance

- Mid-May for the South Entrance to Grant Village and West Thumb; Lake to West Thumb; West Thumb to Old Faithful; Tower Junction to Tower Fall. Cooke City via Colter Pass to the Chief Joseph Scenic Highway intersection to the Long Lake gate opens soon after.

- Mid to late May for the Long Lake Gate over the Beartooth Highway to Red Lodge, Montana, and Tower Fall to Canyon

Fall closures are mid-October for Tower Fall to Canyon Junction and Long Lake via Beartooth Pass to the Montana state line. All other park roads close to the public in early November with the exception of the two roads open year-round.

Additional information on weather and road closings/ conditions can be found as follows:

National Weather Service for both Yellowstone and Grand Teton www.crh.noaa.gov/riw/?n=ynp_gtnp
WYDOT road information 888-WYO-ROAD or www. wyoroad.info/
MTDOT road information 406-444-6200 or www.mdt. mt.gov/travinfo/

For the winter visitor who prefers winter sports, Yellowstone offers a multitude of activity, from snowmobiling and snow coach touring, to cross-country skiing and snowshoeing, to winter ranger-led programs. Yellowstone is a great place to be.

Park concessioners operate lodging, evening programs, snow coach tours, guided ski, snowshoe, snowmobile, and wildlife bus tours. Details can be obtained at the visitor centers, hotel front desks, or by calling Xanterra Parks & Resorts at 307-344-7311. For information on activities originating outside of Yellowstone National Park, call the local chambers of commerce (listed in chapter nine). Remember that most of the roads within the park are not open to wheeled vehicles in winter. Only the road from the North Entrance to Mammoth and the road from the Northeast Entrance west to Mammoth are plowed for wheeled vehicles. All other entrance roads and most of the circle eight road formation (the Grand Loop) that connects the various points of interest in the park are simply groomed for over-snow vehicles in winter. Having said this, the winter grooming of roads is only for certain dates, usually mid-December through mid-March for most roads, late December through March 1 for the East Entrance

Road. Travel over Sylvan Pass along the East Entrance Road is subject to avalanche-related safety delays and closures. Visitors wishing to travel in Yellowstone via snowmobile or snowcoach must either travel by commercial snowcoach or accompany a commercial guide on snowmobiles; private snowcoach and snowmobile use is prohibited, and the park limits the number of both types of vehicles. Contact information for permitted winter service providers can be found at www.nps.gov/yell/planyourvisit/wintbusn.htm.

Cross-country skiing and snowshoeing are both very popular at Yellowstone. Remember that most of Yellowstone is backcountry and many miles of trails are available for skiing. All unplowed roads and trails are available for skiing. When skiing on unplowed roads shared by snowmobiles, keep right to avoid accidents. Remember that you are the person most responsible for your safety. At Yellowstone National Park, you are traveling through wilderness. With this beautiful yet often very lonely experience, you risk weather, hydrothermal areas, deep snow, streams, lakes, avalanches, and very unpredictable wildlife. You are choosing to accept this at your own risk! A Backcountry Use Permit is required for all overnight ski trips. You must contact a park ranger at a ranger station or visitor center before you begin your ski trip.

There are printable ski maps available in pdf form for the Mammoth, Tower, Old Faithful, Northeast, and Canyon areas at www.nps.gov/yell/planyourvisit/skiyell.htm.

Finally, winters at Yellowstone are fierce and severe. You can expose yourself to great danger if you are not prepared with proper attire. Wear many layers, including a windproof and hooded outer layer. Wool or synthetic pants, long underwear, thick wool socks, gloves or wool mittens, and gaiters over boots are all highly recommended for outdoor winter activity at Yellowstone. Wind/rain pants are lightweight and provide extra warmth on windy days. Be sure to wear a facemask-style stocking cap or parka hood when additional protection is needed. Sunscreen is highly recommended; dark sunglasses are a must for sunny days. The glare off the high-altitude snow is much more intense than it is at lower altitudes and can cause snow blindness. More information can be found at www.nps.gov/yell/planyourvisit/winter_equip.htm.

Chapter 15

WILDFIRES

F ires are regular occurrences in any large forest and, in fact, occur in any large national park during the hot and dry periods of the year. They are a necessary and integral part of creating the beauty and landscape. Yes, of course, you do not want to be caught in a fire. You need to be aware of any fires in the area and the fire hazard level, and you must practice fire precautions. However, fire is nature's way of clearing old and dead growth and creating room for new seedlings to sprout and grow.

Years ago, the National Park Service had vastly different protocols for dealing with fire in the parks. They used to do everything in their power to put out fires as quickly as possible. Today, most are allowed to burn under a watchful professional eye, making exceptions to keep them from getting too large and to protect historical buildings and sites in the parks. After decades of the Park Service doing all it could to suppress fire, they eventually realized that allowing naturally occurring fires to burn thins the forests and allows the canopy overhead to open and the needed sunlight to reach lower into the forest.

Fire suppression eventually leads to such a huge buildup of dead and dry timber and bush that eventually lightning or a careless camper will ignite a fire that can grow to horrific and historic levels. This creates a much greater threat to the parks, wildlife, and humans. Have you heard the term "prescribed fires" or "controlled burn?" This refers to the practice of fire professionals intentionally creating fires in sections of a park to eliminate the buildup of dead timber and undergrowth that can greatly intensify wildfires. This keeps the danger of a huge or catastrophic fire at a relatively low level. Park fire professionals also use a process called "mechanical thinning." This means using chain saws to remove certain vegetation, often smaller and less desirable trees, to lessen the chance of fire and to provide safer conditions and better access for firefighters.

Fire allows minerals to be more available for plants by ensuring the release of nutrients from tree wood. It also promotes the weathering of soil minerals, which is especially important in climates like Yellowstone's. Decomposition rates are slower in drier and colder climates than in hot and humid regions. An example of vegetation that has adapted to fire can be found in the lodgepole pines of Yellowstone. These trees produce two types of cones, one of which opens only to release its seedlings at temperatures of at least 113 degrees Fahrenheit. Fire-dependent cones are called serotinous, and ensure that needed seedlings are available after large fires.

The historic Yellowstone fires of 1988 are a prime example of the extensive fire loss that can occur if the buildup of dead forest and underbrush is allowed to accumulate, combined with an equally critical practice of setting limits as to how large to let a natural fire grow to before taking swift action to suppress it's further growth.

These fires burned 793,880 acres within Yellowstone National Park (36 percent of the park), over 1.2 million acres ecosystem wide, and nearly destroyed the historic and irreplaceable Old Faithful Inn. Thank goodness the highly skilled firefighters were able to save the inn.

According to Yellowstone National Park and the National Park Service, in an average year, lightning starts approximately twenty-four fires in Yellowstone NP. Eighty percent of naturally started fires go out on their own. The summer of 1988 was the driest on record up to that time. Humans were responsible for nine fires, while lightning caused forty-two fires in the summer of 1988. These historic fires cost the lives of three hundred large mammals, mostly elk, cost $120 million in fire fighting expenses, and required twenty-five thousand fire-fighting professionals to work the fires. Even with this great and fantastic effort (the largest in U.S. history), it took the critical assistance of heavy rain and snow in the month of September to finally stop the advancing fires.

There is good news from the 1988 fires. Soil fertility, dense and diverse vegetation, and grasslands recovered very quickly. Lodgepole pine forests quickly recovered in the burned areas and aspen reproduction was aided by the fire, which actually stimulated increased growth of suckers from their underground root system. Bear populations were not noticeably affected and many species of cavity-nesting birds found increased suitable habitat due to the resulting dead trees.

In the years since, the various types of forests have made a remarkable recovery on their own due to Mother Nature's fine work. The park service, in analyzing the fire in retrospect and in harvesting all that could be learned from the event, made policy changes. As a result, they no longer put out all the smaller fires that occur naturally. They came to understand that this activity, combined with greater than normal rainfall, had greatly assisted in creating the huge fire source that was just waiting to be ignited. Unfortunately, Mother Nature ignited a historic fire in 1988.

Chapter 16

YELLOWSTONE'S MUST-SEE NEIGHBOR: GRAND TETON NATIONAL PARK

O ne of my all-time favorite movies also provided my first visions of the Teton Range and the beautiful winding Snake River: *Spencer's Mountain*. This fantastic movie from 1963, starred Henry Fonda, Maureen O'Hara, and James MacArthur (Danno from *Hawaii Five-O*). If you have never seen it, I highly recommend it. "Spencer's Mountain" inspired the movie *Walton's Mountain*, which inspired *The Walton's* TV series. Anyway, as the beginning credits roll, the background scene is Grand Teton National Park, the Teton Range, and the Snake River. Much of the movie was filmed in Grand Teton NP. It is probably a better advertisement for the beauty of this park than any they ever intentionally paid for. Anyway, I actually know a family who traveled to Yellowstone NP for a week all the way from Indiana, yet failed to visit Grand Teton NP. The wife wanted to, but the husband and kids said they had no interest. I have to believe they simply had no idea what they were turning down.

Here, I want to share but a few thoughts on what is one of our country's greatest national parks in its own right. In 2008, Grand Teton NP was the ninth most visited national park in the United States with the National Park Service officially listing visitation at 2,485,987. It is located just seven and a half miles directly south of Yellowstone NP along the John D. Rockefeller Jr. Memorial Parkway; this section of road is closed to wheeled vehicles in winter. The entire parkway runs eighty-two miles from the West Thumb Basin in Yellowstone NP south through Grand Teton NP to its south entrance and the town of Jackson Hole, Wyoming.

Grand Teton NP has so much to see that it can easily fill an entire vacation all by itself and is not the type of thing you can see in a half day on your way to or from Yellowstone. However, if you have extra time on your tip to Yellowstone, read on. If you fear that you will never be in this part of the country again, you'll want to be able to say that you have been to Grand Teton National Park.

Yellowstone and Grand Teton go together like Minneapolis goes with Saint Paul, or Dallas goes with Fort Worth. To make a more appropriate national park analogy, they go together like Sequoia and Kings Canyon national parks. They are inseparable; at the same time, they are also very different.

Having mentioned earlier that Yellowstone was our country's, and the world's first national park, I will go out on a limb and credit Grand Teton as our country's nineteenth national park (subject to disagreement, as many of our national parks have had their boundaries and designations changed throughout the years, making chronological rankings an inexact science), established on February 26, 1929. Through the generosity of John D. Rockefeller, acreage was added later, creating the 485-square-mile park as it is today in 1950. Grand Teton is known for many things, obviously the Teton Range, but also for beautiful lakes and wildlife. In fact, after describing all the wonderful wildlife in Yellowstone, actually, Grand Teton has often been judged to be the best National Park in the entire national park system for wildlife viewing. This park is a great place to see pronghorn, elk, deer, coyote, moose, and many other animals. The shallow marshlands that exist on both sides of the Snake River provide a fantastic place to view Moose.

Grand Teton is a tremendous park for hiking. I would much rather hike here than in Yellowstone. Don't get me wrong; the hiking in Yellowstone is terrific and varied. There are so many miles of hikes that you can return time after time and never repeat a trail. However, in Yellowstone you hike mostly for what is available to see at the end of the trail and only available via the trail. There are geysers, meadows, waterfalls, and backcountry that can be accessed only via a good hearty hike. However, in Grand Teton, the hiking is mostly up and down her majestic mountains. I, personally, like strenuous hikes consisting of great incline and decline. All of Grand Teton's great peaks, Grand Teton (from which the park gets its name), Owen, Teewinot, Middle Teton, South Teton, and others have great hiking trails that take you to views for miles around and to several small pristine alpine lakes. As you hike, you quickly notice the elevation gain and the increasing distance you can see looking mostly east from the range. The forests and their fresh smells quickly take you from the trailhead below to a land where stress, worries, the modern world, and the job you are vacationing from are soon but a distant memory. Take a backpack full of good food, energy bars, and plenty of water, and plan to sweat the day away generating a memory that will last you a lifetime!

The Jenny Lake area is a must-see. Allocate the time to catch the boat that leaves three times an hour from the south end of Jenny Lake. The boat takes you to the other side of Jenny Lake to hike the Cascade Canyon Trail. A short half-mile walk takes you to Hidden Falls or a full-mile walk takes you to Inspiration Point for an overlook of the entire lake. If you want to experience the entire trail, it travels a full seven miles for increasing better and better views (nine and a half miles if you skip the boat and walk along the shore of Jenny Lake rather than cross on the boat).

Another great hike is the Amphitheater Lake Trail with its trailhead at Lupine Meadows. This is a nine-mile, very strenuous round-trip, with an elevation climb of 2,960 feet for breathtaking views of Jackson Hole at an elevation of 9,698 feet. Plan on at least six hours on the trail and leave early enough in the day so you do not risk darkness before you return.

Grand Teton's Cathedral Group (Mt. Teewinot, Grand Teton, and Mt. Owen)

Besides hiking, Grand Teton NP offers climbing, backpacking, fishing, boating (motorboats permitted on Jenny Lake, 10 horsepower max., and Jackson Lake), swimming in all lakes (but highly discouraged in the Snake River), biking, and more. Non-motorized boating is permitted on Jackson, Jenny, Phelps, Emma Matilda, Two Ocean, Taggart, Bradley, Bearpaw, Leigh, and String lakes. Sailboats, water skiing, and windsurfing are allowed only on Jackson Lake. Only non-motorized floating crafts including canoes, rafts, dories, and kayaks are allowed on the Snake River within the park boundary and along the parkway.

Grand Teton NP is officially open all year, although most facilities, including most lodging locations, close for the winter season. The main road through the park, the outer highway 26/89/191 is open year-round within the park, but the Teton Park Road is closed to wheeled vehicles from early November through late April. During this time, the road is open for non-motorized use (skiing, snowshoeing, cycling, walking, etc.). The Craig Thomas Discovery and Visitor Center is open 364 days a year (closed Christmas Day). The winter activities here, such as snowshoeing and cross-country skiing are terrific; however, as is the case in Yellowstone, this is primarily a summer destination.

Activities are varied and, for the most part, very similar to Yellowstone with hiking, fishing, boating, camping, majestic wildlife, ranger programs, etc. There are even ranger-led moonlit snowshoe hikes on specific dates featuring a full moon. However, while similar in these arenas, every national park is unique. I find all of them well worth visiting.

For additional information on Grand Teton National Park, call general park visitor information at 307-739-3300, lodging and camping information at 307-739-3603, weather information at 307-739-3611, or Road Conditions at 307-739-3682, or visit the park's Web site at www.nps.gov/grte/.

Chapter 17

FINAL THOUGHTS

Many people might say that the distinction of Yellowstone is that it was our country's, and the world's very first national park. While it is true that it was the first, the true distinction lies in postulating as to why it got this distinction. There are many, many great national parks. Even if you choose the best of the best, you still can't choose one that is definitively the best. Every "national park-er" will have his or her favorite. You can make an argument based upon personal preference for so many parks, and those that get mentioned the most often include Yellowstone, Yosemite, Grand Canyon, Glacier, Denali, Zion, and more. There are many smaller and lesser known national parks that I love to make the argument for including Bryce Canyon and Crater Lake to mention just two. However, the argument that Yellowstone is often thought of as the best just because it was the first may be another example of the chicken or the egg argument.

Yellowstone is the second-largest national park in the contiguous forty-eight United States and covers parts of three states. Yellowstone has the greatest variety of wildlife of any national park. It is the only place on earth to have wild bison continually present since primitive times. Yellowstone has one of the largest grizzly bear populations in the lower forty-eight United States, one of the largest concentrations of elk in the entire world, and contains all the large animal species known to be present here when Europeans first arrived. There are more thermal features here than anywhere else in the world, estimated at half the world's total. The main section of the park sits on top of one of the largest volcanoes in the world. The Lower Falls of the Yellowstone River, at 308 feet, is one of the highest waterfalls in North America. Yellowstone Lake is the largest high-altitude lake in North America. Yellowstone has multiple historic hotels and offers an abundance of recreational activities. Elevations range from 5,282 feet at Reese Creek to 11,358 feet at Eagle Peak, and the park covers a total area larger than the states of Rhode Island and Delaware combined. This magnificent place represents and provides a trip back in time, a look at all that is too often lost in today's rush-hour, crime-infested, big-city life. Yellowstone offers as grand a family experience as you will ever experience with your children. Believe me, as one who treasures the memories and photo albums of our trips to this fabulous place, with children who are presently sixteen and fourteen years of age, I know the family trips remaining are numbered and I would not trade our decisions to visit this place and to visit it multiple times for anything.

Yellowstone is like falling in love, riding a bike, or having a child. Visiting at least once is one of the items that should be on the short list of things you must do in your lifetime. So, back to that chicken or the egg thing. Maybe Yellowstone National Park should not be thought of as the best because it was the first; maybe it simply was the first because it is the best?

Appendix A

MISSELLANEOUS NATIONAL PARK TIPS

Book early! Book your trip, and especially your lodging, as far in advance as possible, preferably six to twelve months. Due to limited availability and very reasonable pricing, cabins and other accommodations within the national parks rarely display a vacancy sign. Do not be under the misperception that there are chain motels within U.S. National Parks or that the lodging just outside the parks is convenient. Driving two or more hours round-trip to a hotel located outside the park will take much of the fun out of your trip. Book early. Ask questions about proximity to the main attractions, and have an unbelievable experience.

Stay in the park, if at all possible. It is part of the park experience to awaken in the park and walk out your cabin door to see the waterfalls or wildlife. Staying at a chain hotel is something you do when going to the beach or an amusement park, not a national park!

Consider taking your trip in the off-season. Parks are most crowded in the summer; still nothing compares to the crowds at other types of vacation destinations. However, if you travel in the fall or spring, you will have a much more relaxed time. Because of lessened crowds, you will see more wildlife. Also, you should not have to wait for a table at dinner. Finally, you will see stronger flowing waterfalls in spring or unbelievable fall color— and you will save money!

Attend as many evening ranger programs as possible. They are free, very informative, relaxing, and appropriate for the entire family. Besides, what else are you going to be doing without television or radio? That's right; most parks do not receive television or radio signals (no Internet either).

Take a deck of cards. While it is common to turn in early, due to all the exercise of walking or hiking during the day plus the relaxing effect of the fresh park air, you still need to occupy the early evening. Basically, you have two options for entertainment: attend the afore mentioned ranger programs or bring your own entertainment.

Stop prior to entering the national park and purchase snacks. You can find soft drinks and snacks within the parks, but often the General Stores there have higher prices, close early, and offer a limited selection. Stopping in the last town or at the last gas/food mart will be a move you will be glad you made.

Never hike without water and food. You can always spot the novice (been there, done that). They are the ones three miles down a trail, sweating profusely, carrying a warm twelve-ounce plastic bottle of spring water, and asking questions like, "How much farther do I have to go?" Why risk your life—or even not getting the most enjoyment out of a hike—by not being prepared? There is nothing macho about proving you can do a trail without refreshment. You need to get a backpack of some sort and have sufficient water (preferably cold, as with a CamelBak®) and food (at least energy bars, if not a sandwich). Remember, you only paid around $25 to get your entire family into the park for a full seven days. You certainly have enough money left for a backpack!

Heed the advice on wildlife. If you do, you'll be fine and have experiences you'll treasure for a lifetime. You have very little to fear if you use common sense. First of all, you may not see a bear. Second, if you do, they are more afraid of you than you are of them. If you keep your distance and learn what to do if one should come toward you, you'll be fine.

I will never forget two things I have been told that really taught me the ins and outs of wildlife. At Yellowstone, a ranger told me about the German tourist who asked his wife to take his picture while he put his arm around a bison. STUPID, right? It killed him. At Jasper NP in Alberta, Canada, a ranger stated that there have been more tourists killed by falling trees than by bears. In other words, be informed, act accordingly, and enjoy the kind of fabulous trip that only the national parks can provide.

Money-saving tips. Eat breakfast in your room or cabin. You can get milk, juice, fruit, and pastries in the general store. This way, you pay for only two meals out each day.

Not to confuse anyone here: food at national parks is cheap compared to the usual vacation destinations. Do not expect to set aside a Disney World type food budget for this trip. At the same time, while most meals are very reasonable, it always pays to inquire ahead.

For example, at Yosemite, the famous and breathtaking Ahwahnee Hotel has a dining room that is not to miss. However, prices here are slightly higher than most other parks' best dining, and higher than other options in Yosemite. Also, the dining room has a "resort casual" dress code for dinner. Resort casual means collared shirts and long pants for men, and dresses, skirts/slacks, and blouses, or evening pants suits for women that will probably not be used at any other time on the trip. Who wants to have to pack a required outfit with limited suitcase space and airlines charging for each piece of checked baggage? Why not plan to have breakfast or lunch in the dining room? It is much cheaper. You can easily get in without a reservation, and it will allow you to experience eating in the same historic dining room.

Buy a photo album at a gift store within the park that has the name of the park on the outside. You will need to buy one anyway. Also, take a picture of your family by the park entrance sign. Every national park has a cool sign at each entrance, which makes for the ideal first photo in your picture album.

Buy your film, digital camera photo card, batteries, and an extra set of batteries at home. They may not have exactly what you need at the park, and even if they do, you will pay the captive audience pricing.

Appendix B

DAY HIKING ESSENTIALS

You need someone to hike with. Resist, if possible, the urge to hike alone.

Backpack

CamelBak® and Water: Carry at least 150 percent of what you think you'll need. A CamelBak® maintains ice in your water for hours.

Food: Carry more than you think you'll need, and more than just lunch.
   *Sandwich: Keep the sandwich dry until the time you actually eat it. Add condiments when ready to eat.
   *Salty items: Nuts and chips, Pringles® carry especially well due to container protecting them from getting crushed.
   *Fruit
   *Energy bars, like Powerbar®

Trail Map

Hiking Boots

Thick Socks: Prevent those nasty blisters.

Compact Binoculars

Compass

Hat

Sunscreen

Insect Repellant

Bear Bell: This is almost always a good idea and is highly recommended at Yosemite, Rocky Mountain, Sequoia, Kings Canyon, Yellowstone, Grand Teton, Smoky Mountain, and a MUST at Glacier and all Alaska NPs.

Camera: Carry a disposable on the more challenging hikes. It's lighter, and there's no risk of breaking a good camera due to tough trails or late day fatigue.

Cell Phone: Do not rely on coverage.

Understanding Your Trail: How difficult is the rating? How much time does it normally take to complete? Are there any facilities along the way? How many hours of daylight do you have left?

Understanding the Weather Forecast: You do not want to be on exposed and high rock during lightning. Also, you will need to understand the temperature expectations for differing times of the day. During certain times of the year, especially spring and fall, you will want to layer clothing. This will allow you to keep warm in the colder morning and evening periods, yet allow you to shed layers during the relatively warmer midday!

Hiking Permit: This is not usually required for day hiking, but it is the norm for overnight hiking.

Flashlight

Rain Gear

Bear Spray: This is highly recommended in select national parks (Yellowstone, Grand Teton, Glacier, most Alaska national parks, and others) where there are large populations of bear, especially grizzly bear, and where the park encourages and allows bear spray to be carried.

Appendix C

SECTIONAL ROAD MAPS

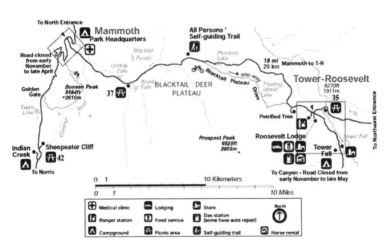

Mammoth to Tower–Roosevelt

175

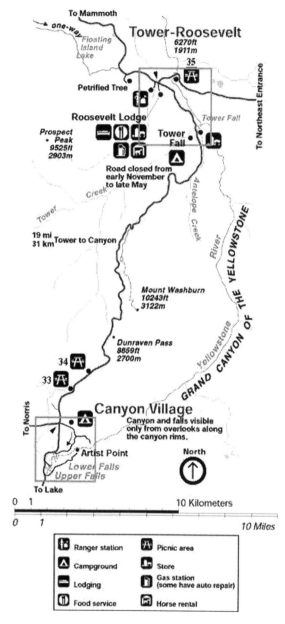

Canyon Village to Tower–Roosevelt

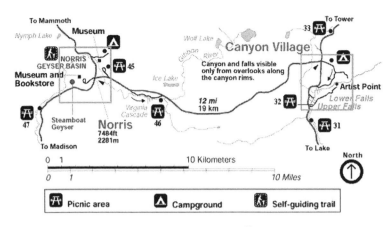

Norris to Canyon Village

Mammoth Hot Springs to Norris

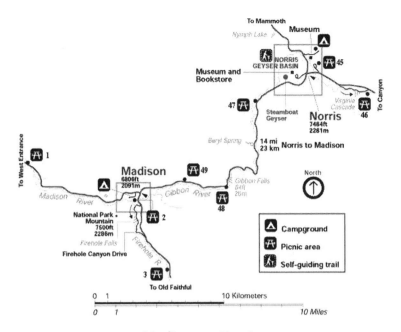

To Mammoth

Museum

Nymph Lake

NORRIS
GEYSER BASIN

Museum and
Bookstore

45

To Canyon

*Virginia
Cascade*

47

Steamboat
Geyser

Norris
7484ft
2281m

46

To West Entrance

Madison   River

1

Beryl Spring

14 mi
23 km Norris to Madison

North

Madison
6806ft
2091m

49

Gibbon   River

*Gibbon Falls
84ft
26m*

48

National Park
Mountain
7500ft
2286m

2

Firehole Falls

Firehole Canyon Drive

Firehole   R.

3

To Old Faithful

▲	Campground
🅰	Picnic area
🅰	Self-guiding trail

0   1   10 Kilometers

0   1   10 Miles

Madison to Norris

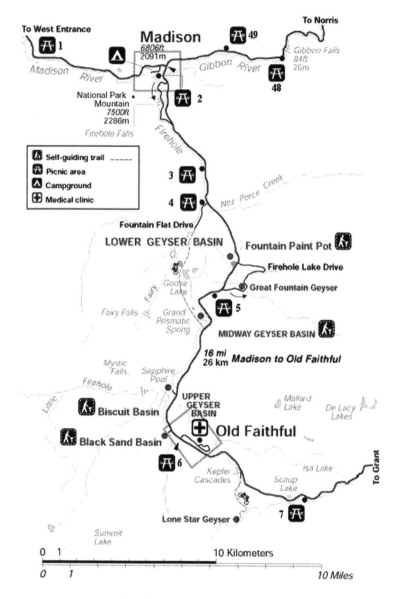

Madison to Old Faithful

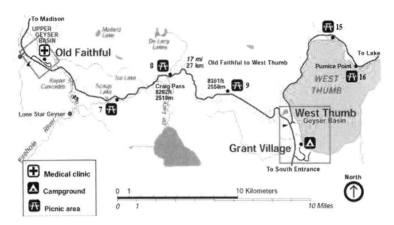

Old Faithful to West Thumb and Grant Village

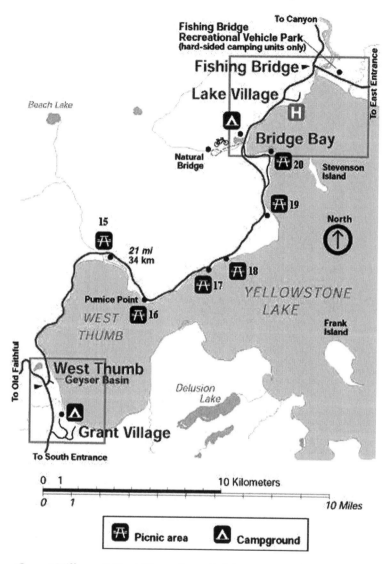

Grant Village/West Thumb to Bridge Bay/Lake Village/
Fishing Bridge

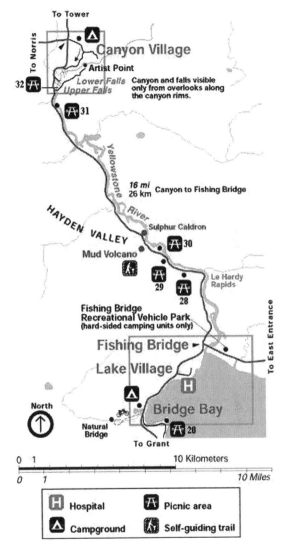

Bridge Bay/Lake Village/Fishing Bridge to
Canyon Village

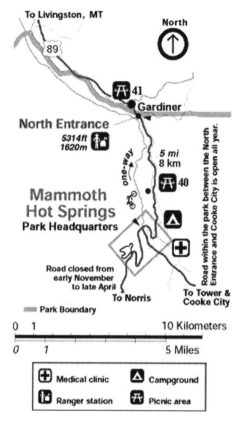

North Entrance to Mammoth Hot Springs

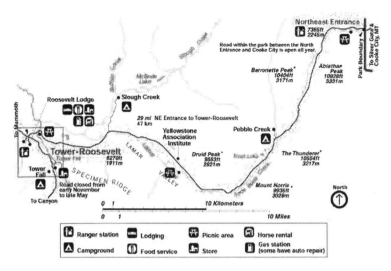

Tower–Roosevelt to Northeast Entrance

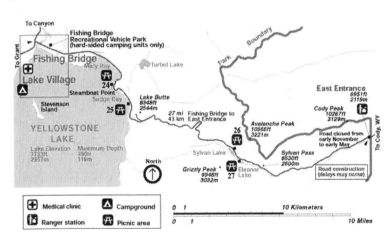

East Entrance to Fishing Bridge

185

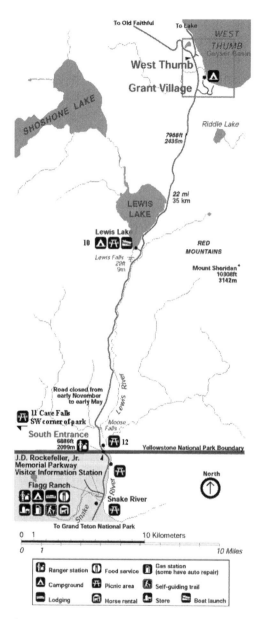

South Entrance to Grant Village/West Thumb

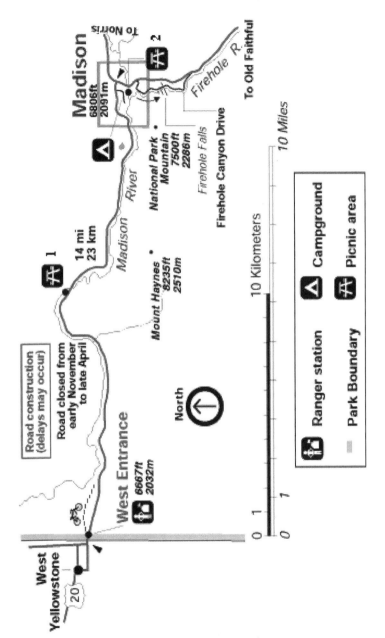

West Entrance to Madison

Finally, I wish to thank the National Park Service and Yellowstone National Park for some of the absolutely best family vacations, best moments, best days, and best memories of my entire life!

INDEX

9737799R0

Made in the USA
Lexington, KY
24 May 2011